The Glad Hand

First published 1979 by Pluto Press Limited
Unit 10 Spencer Court, 7 Chalcot Road, London NW1 8LH

Copyright © Snoo Wilson 1979

All rights whatsoever in this play are strictly reserved and applications for
permission to perform it in whole or in part must be made in advance, before
rehearsals begin, to Goodwin Associates, 12 Upper Addison Gardens,
London W14

Pluto Press gratefully acknowledges financial assistance from the
Calouste Gulbenkian Foundation, Lisbon, with the publication of this series

ISBN 0 86104 212 3

Designed by Tom Sullivan
Cover designed by Claudine Meissner
Printed in Great Britain by Latimer Trend & Company Ltd Plymouth

Snoo Wilson

The Glad Hand

Pluto  Plays

The Glad Hand

When this play finally got on stage, there was an exhibition of Piranesi's etchings including the dungeon, or 'Carceri' series, one of which had formed the inspiration for the setting of the play, which is inside an oil tanker. Neither I nor the designer nor the audience had ever been inside one, but I wanted to create some kind of modern equivalent of those huge gothic prisons, where the architects' figures struggle up never-ending staircases. But I am a playwright not an architect and I would like to have people as the centre of the drama: beyond the first five minutes the actors should really be winning the contest of attention between them and the set unless the play is quite anaesthetic.

I had carried Piranesi's etching inside me for fifteen years, although I had forgotten his name. The intention of the etching is to correspond to and inspire the imagination to see and feel what does not exist, and the machinery of theatre is similar. We enter into imaginative conspiracy, about what is not there, rather than what is. The actors however have to produce this magic from the premise of everyday life. But as magic has this, too, as its background (only the most facetious still can consign it to wizards with pointy hats) it should be possible to demonstrate both its plausibility, and the premise that the strange and miraculous have sources in ourselves, since humanity is the source and measure of all the passion and action on stage.

The structure of the play relies on a manic fascist whose insensitivity and idealism and conspiracy theories were kissed into life by the author's own, but the play is not a *Roman à clé*, although I did steal parts of Marylin from a friend. I hope, to the extent that I feel uneasy about my introduction, that Shakespeare's rule of thumb (a good wine needs no bush) does not work in reverse, and that these few words act as an extraneous hurdle to fell potential readers whose glance has fallen on the shelf space between Barbara Windsor and Sandy Wilson. Ladies, gentlemen, and Bernard Shaw—*The Glad Hand*.

Snoo Wilson

The Glad Hand was first produced at the Royal Court Theatre on 11 May 1978. The cast was as follows:

Ritsaat	Antony Sher
Lazarus	Olivier Pierre
Carson	Julian Hough
Bill Hooley	Tony Rohr
Brian Hooley	Alan Devlin
Kathleen Hooley	Rachel Bell
Marylin	Julie Walters
Sylvia Hooley	Di Patrick
Marks	Nicholas le Prevost
Wishbone	Will Knightley
Umberto	Thomas Baptiste
Clements	Manning Redwood
Willya	Gwyneth Strong

Directed by Max Stafford-Clark
Designed by Peter Hartwell

A NOTE ON THE AUTHOR

Snoo Wilson received the John Whiting Award for 1978 for *The Glad Hand*, his seventh full-length play. Others include *The Pleasure Principle*, performed at the Royal Court in 1973, published by Eyre Methuen; *Pignight* and *Blowjob* published by John Calder (Publishers) Ltd; *Vampire* for Portable Theatre, *The Beast* for the Royal Shakespeare Company, *The Everest Hotel*, all of which have been published in *Plays and Players*. *Soul of the White Ant* is published by TQ Publications Ltd. The stage version of *A Greenish Man* is also published by Pluto Press.

ACT I

SCENE 1

The inside of an oil tanker.

The stage is a platform. The rear wall begins to curve under as it meets it. Big welded support beam. A pyramid upstage, five-foot base, suspended above a bed. Canvas on board flooring, stained with pigeon-shit. Overhead, centre, a super-market TV monitor. A ladder leading up into the dark, upstage. Suggestion of vast spaces above and below, dwarfing humanity.

LAZARUS, *a fat screenwriter in gumboots and dressing-gown, is seated on an empty beer-crate right centre, eating a bowl of porridge.* MRS HOOLEY *up right with her tea trolley.* MARKS *and* WISHBONE *enter from up left.* WISHBONE *moves to the trolley to collect their tea and porridge, as* MARKS *sets their folding canvas chairs and beer-crate 'table' down left.*

Mrs Hooley Morning, boys.

Marks
Wishbone }Good morning, Mrs Hooley.

Mrs Hooley What were you doing last night?

Wishbone We were having a meeting about not being able to receive post or newspapers. Why weren't you there?

Mrs Hooley Well, I've got all my family here, so there's no-one to write to me. And I never bother with newspapers.

Marks Yes, well . . . what about the rest of us?

Lazarus (*looking up from his porridge*) This is disgusting. Why is there no proper food at breakfast? This fucking porridge is *burnt*. You actors must be used to better conditions than this, aren't you?

Marks (*joins* WISHBONE *down left*) Well?

Wishbone I'd have to taste it to make sure, but I think it's probably Crewe Rep. nineteen sixty-four . . . *As You Like It.*

Marks Well done. Now the tea.

Wishbone Farnham nineteen sixty-two.

Both *Mrs Warren's Profession.*

Marks Bang on.

> *They sit, with* WISHBONE *in the onstage chair.*
>
> MRS HOOLEY *moves towards the up left exit.* LAZARUS *follows.*

Lazarus Mrs Hooley! Mrs Hooley!

Mrs Hooley What is it now?

Lazarus Did you get me coffee? Remember I asked for coffee in the morning? I don't drink tea, it makes me throw up.

Mrs Hooley Everyone else drinks tea. Mr Marks . . . Mr Wishbone . . .

Lazarus They are actors. They are British. I am none of these things. I am a writer and an artist. I have an ulcer. I will not drink tea.

Mrs Hooley I'll see what I can do. (*Exits up left.*)

Wishbone She gone to get you coffee?

Lazarus (*collecting more porridge*) She doesn't know what she's doing, what's going on. (*Returns to seat*) If we *do* make a stand against Ritsaat, it's got to be unanimous. *Complete* withdrawal of labour. Not having her tottering around making him tea. And you know what? That guy Ritsaat can't admit he's gay. He's got a whole tanker full of fags. He's got a *block*.

Wishbone What about your own block?

Marks Yes. Any chance of seeing a script yet?

Lazarus I do not have a block!

Marks Definitely Farnham nineteen sixty-two.

RITSAAT *enters up left.*

Piss. (*Throws tea on floor between them, turns, sees* RITSAAT.) Oh! Sorry, Ritsaat. I think one of your pigeons must have shat in the tea.

Ritsaat They're not pigeons – they're doves. I wanted passenger pigeons, like they had in the old West. I tried to get this bloke to breed them back, but he said too much recent radiation had twisted and warped the genetic code. Time is running out. (*To* LAZARUS.) How's the writing going, Lazarus?

Lazarus (*rises*) Terrific.

Ritsaat You know we're nearly inside the Bermuda Triangle – so anything could happen. You have to be prepared.

MARKS *and* WISHBONE *rise to left of* RITSAAT.

Marks Mr Ritsaat – something to ask you. Suppose we do get into a time-warp in the middle of the Bermuda Triangle, like you plan . . .

Ritsaat Yes.

Marks And suppose we all get moved back to eighteen eighty-six, like you want . . .

Ritsaat I'm the only one who's going back to have a shoot-out with the AntiChrist.

Wishbone But if we come along by accident to eighteen eighty-six . . .

Marks Yes, we ought to get this straightened out now.

Wishbone Until we get back to the present day, we'd be due for overtime, wouldn't we?

Marks Very roughly, a hundred years' overtime.

Ritsaat Very funny. Time isn't a straight line.

Wishbone Overtime is.

Ritsaat No . . . the past and the future take place in an infinite house behind locked doors. The present is the corridor. I'm employing you to unpick the locks. I step through, the doors close, and you pick up your pay when you get back to Liverpool. (*Breaks right.*) Why do you eat so much, Lazarus?

Lazarus I . . .

Ritsaat Don't you know? (*Exits down right.*)

BILL HOOLEY *enters up left, to tea trolley.* LAZARUS *breaks down right.*

Lazarus I could *kill* him.

Bill Why don't you?

BILL *helps himself to tea.*

Lazarus Look, this is going to have to stop. This fascist asshole with his jack-boots is trampling all over us!

Bill (*in send-up voice*) Morning, boys.

Marks
Wishbone } Morning, Bill.

Bill Somebody made a pig's ear of unblocking that lavatory.

MRS HOOLEY *enters up left, moves towards tea trolley.*

Mother, you do it.

Mrs Hooley Will I do what?

Bill The bog's blocked.

Lazarus It's no good asking her. She won't do anything.

Bill You have to ask her right. (*To* MRS HOOLEY.) You old slag! Go and unblock the fucking toilet!

Mrs Hooley That's no way to speak to your mother.

Bill It's what you're here for, isn't it?

MRS HOOLEY *collects mop and bucket from up right.*

Lazarus (*rises*) Wait! The coffee . . .

Mrs Hooley You wouldn't speak to me like that if you loved me. (*Exit up left with mop and bucket.*)

Bill She's a right lazy old bugger. (*Moves to left.*) Marks, was it you that blocked the bog again?

Marks I admit the soft impeachment.

Bill If it was soft, there'd be no trouble.

Marks I just need some fruit, that is all.

BRIAN *enters up left with a cardboard box, crosses towards down right.*

Brian, are there any apples?

BRIAN *exits down right.* MARKS *calls after him.*

Ritsaat said there were apples.

Lazarus We'll be lucky to get dog-biscuits in a week! Bill, do your parents know what they are doing? Like, do they know we exist, we have appetites, we live and breathe? Coffee! I've seen it on the shelves – once. We had it. It was terrific. You just have to boil some water!

CLEMENTS *enters up right, to tea trolley, pours tea.*

I know the Irish have an aversion to the culinary art, but these granules you do not even have to cook!

BRIAN, *without box, recrosses from down right.* BILL *sits on the bench right and begins to eat.* MARKS *stands in front of* BRIAN *at centre, blocking him.*

Marks Brian – old chap. Do you think we could score an apple?
Brian But nobody likes apples.

Lazarus
Marks } (*fortissimo*)
Wishbone } Yes they do!

Brian I'll see what I can do. (*Exits up left.*)

WILLYA *enters up left, to tea trolley, takes porridge.*

ALL *return to their seats.*

Willya Has the Third World War broken out, like Ritsaat said?
Wishbone It's been indefinitely postponed, for lack of a script.

CLEMENTS *moves down right with his tea.*

Willya That's not what you said, Lazarus. You said you had an idea.
Lazarus I do. It's terrific. Ritsaat will hate it.
Willya What is it?
Lazarus Bill gets his legs chopped off.
Bill What for?
Lazarus Being a communist agitator.

CARSON *enters up left, moves to* CLEMENTS. WILLYA *sits with* BILL *on bench right.*

Carson Hi, Clem—how you doing?
Clements Do you have anything for reducing the sexual urges of healthy forty-year-old males, Carson?
Carson Get Mrs Hooley to give you a mercy fuck.
Clements It's her granddaughter I'm after. I'm in love with a thirteen-year-old nymphet, and I can't wait to sink my teeth into her tight little butt.
Carson (*pause*) Is that the problem?
Clements Jail is the problem.

LAZARUS *rises, moves to tea trolley, leaves porridge bowl, pours tea.*

Carson Well, her old man's been poking her for years, and he gets away with it.
Clements Oh, that's the way? Hell, I've been married six times, and I never stayed with them long enough to see the daughters grow up.

Carson He's not her real father.

Clements The dirty bastard. I suppose that was why he brought her on the boat.

Carson Listen, d'you fancy earning a few bob?

Clements How much is that in dollars?

Carson Say twenty-five?

LAZARUS *sits on crate up right centre, works on his script.*

Clements Doing what?

Carson See, I rather oversold myself, and I asked for double money, saying I was a psychic surgeon. Well, I know sod-all about it, except for a bit of reading. But if you said you were ill, I could sort of cure you – know what I mean? – for . . . fifty dollars.

MRS HOOLEY *enters up left, moves to tea trolley.*

Clements What do I have to do – parade around drinking your astrological herb teas?

Carson No. We say you've got a hypothermic cancer. We'll do a cod operation, and then we'll stick you under the pyramid for a couple of days.

Clements How does a hundred dollars sound?

Carson Without my calculator . . . all right.

Clements Good old hippy capitalism.

Carson You'd better do some research into being ill. And if you played your cards right, the girl of your dreams could come up and stroke your fevered brow, while you sweated it out in there.

Clements Will you get her for me?

Carson I can ask her.

Clements OK. It'll be more fun than standing around all day, waiting for that fat fag commie to finish blackening American history. Couldn't I have something a little less terminal?

MARKS *returns the empty porridge bowls to the trolley, collects two more teas.*

Carson No, sorry. Not for my professional reputation.

Clements OK. I tell you, boy, the CIA should never have got involved in this. (*Pause, looks round.*) That's where I'm from. The CIA. And it's not the first time they've invested in occult attempts at time travel. Would you believe this is the first job I ever carried a shooter? 'Just in case you get through to eighteen eighty-six, and can't get back.' They're trying to get rid of me.

Carson (*to himself*) CIA . . . I never thought I'd build a replica of the ancient wisdom with CIA money. Bad vibes, man – very bad vibes.

Clements This whole trip is a bad apple.

RITSAAT, *enters up right, moves to up centre, rings ship's bell, down to centre.*

Ritsaat Come on, everybody – finish your breakfast and listen to this!

All scurry to listen. BRIAN *enters up left, moves to centre.* CARSON *moves, at a beckoning gesture from* RITSAAT, *to right of him.*

Please sit down, everybody.

They do so.

We've been cruising, now, for six months. Six months of valuable time, while all around us the world situation got worse. Communists, setting up puppet governments all over Africa – and for every one of those six months, a Russian nuclear submarine has been launched, each one with sufficient capacity to destroy the cities of the West. How long do we have to wait for Armageddon? All we know is, that this time there isn't going to be any winners. The First World War is going to look like a tea-party at Bloomsbury compared to this. This will be what the strategists call a 'two to the ninth' conflict: a war with two thousand million dead. And there it is – the coming victory of the AntiChrist . . . unless *we* can stop him. (*Moves among them.*) You are all doing work that is crucial to the survival of the human race as we know it. But when will he come? To meet him in the future will be already too late – so we've got to go back. All we have to do is traverse the short distance which divides us from the recent known appearance of the AntiChrist that I have chosen: the Cowboy Strike in Wyoming in eighteen eighty-six. We have to tap the Caucasian memory to find the model of those times. And when we have found it, he will have to come again. In fact, I don't think he's going to have any bloody choice. (*Return to centre.*) But the formation of this model, this template, is up to Lazarus – who, as we all know, still has a block. So this morning, we are going to try something slightly different.

CARSON *whispers to* RITSAAT, *then he and* WILLYA *exit down left.*

Clements is ill – you've all seen him getting sicker. He's got cancer. Now none of you know, but Carson is a psychic surgeon. I've called you to watch the cure, a victory of inspiration and genius over baser beliefs – I hope it'll help us all in our work. (*Starts applause.*)

WILLYA *wheels on the pyramid from down left, and is followed by* CARSON, *now wearing a robe and carrying a Bowie knife.* WILLYA *sits* CLEMENTS *under the pyramid, at centre.*

Clements (*pause*) Hold it, boy – you look stoned.
Carson Don't worry, Clements. There are interfaces, see, between the astral and the physical body, where the psychic surgeon goes in with his rusty old knife – and draws out the malignant cells through the ectoplasm.
Clements Ritsaat, should we be operating if he's stoned?

Carson (*raising the knife*) Lie down! I'm not stoned – I'm *tripping*. And I'm crazed with this terrible bloodlust, too, if you must know.

Clements No – you don't understand! I've got a weak heart! My pills – they're back in my cabin –

Ritsaat Hold him down!

BRIAN *and* MRS HOOLEY *hold him down. A circle has begun to form around the pyramid.*

Clements Carson – stop! I'm going to die of fright, if I don't die of germs. Carson! That knife is filthy. I come from a clean country!

Carson (*trancelike*) I can't hear you!

Brian Settle down. Mr Carson's the seventh son of a seventh son. He's a healer.

Carson Yeah, some of the cats in Brazil, they don't even use a knife. They just use their hands to tear out the cancer. And – *MUSIC!* lights!

CLEMENTS *faints.* WILLYA *moves up centre and switches on the music: Electric Light Orchestra's 'Mister Kingdom'. Lights to purple.* CARSON *produces the ectoplasm, seemingly from* CLEMENT'*s stomach, slowly, perfectly. A superb show.*

(*Pause.*) Absolute quiet . . . concentration . . . (*Uses hands to 'cure'* CLEMENTS.)

Bill (*pause*) 'Life was never the same when we got our miracle microwave oven.'

Carson What do you know about pyramidology, Bill? What do any of you know? The pyramid is a shape which is the repository of all the knowledge of the ancients contained in its perfect proportions. Consider it's calculated beauty. You can find the expression of Pi, the proof of all geometry, from this shape. It's perfect, I tell you. More perfect than man will ever be . . .

Clements (*interrupting*) Something's happening . . . I'm getting something . . . I'm out of the body . . .

Ritsaat Carson – stop a minute. Let him talk a minute.

Carson D'you want me to stop now?

Wishbone He said he was getting something –

Carson He's not getting anything for this – honest.

Ritsaat Turn that music down!

Carson All right, all right. But I need a bit of atmosphere to work in.

WILLYA *exits down right and turns off the music.* RITSAAT *bends over* CLEMENTS, *who is now in a real trance.*

Ritsaat Clements . . . are you there? . . . (CLEMENTS *grunts.*) What's the date where you are?

Clements Winter.

Ritsaat What do you see?

Clements White woman. They piled the bodies in the snow.
Ritsaat Who?
Clements We did . . . the cavalry. White woman . . . living with the Indians.
Hidden among the bodies with her wain.
Ritsaat And then?
Clements (*another incarnation*) There is mother under the oleanders . . .
There is someone there with her. Yes – I had a sister. Open the window
. . . it is getting dark. (*A great shudder.*)
Ritsaat (*pause*) Clements, listen. We need names, dates, places.

CLEMENTS *starts to pant, fast and shallow.*

Carson Wow. Look at that!
Ritsaat Have you see anything like that?
Carson It's third-stage labour breathing, that is.

CLEMENTS *stops. Pause.*

There is a terrific crash offstage.

Ritsaat What's that?

The onstage speakers start buzzing and whining suddenly.

Carson Don't worry, it's – er – just a synchronistic event.

The speakers pack up with a pop.

Oh, shit!
Ritsaat What's the matter?
Carson Blown out the speakers! Cunt's blown out the speakers! I paid two
hundred quid for them!
Ritsaat What cunt?
Carson *I* dunno.

CARSON *has become worried.*

Ritsaat Aren't you going to carry on?
Carson I can't, with me equipment being busted up.
Ritsaat What by? Is it a sympathetic psychic event?
Carson I don't know what it is.
Marks Mr Ritsaat, why don't you go and see what the noise was?
Carson I can't carry on. I'm upset. (*Exits right.*)
Wishbone It *was* rather a large bang.
Marks Yes, suppose it *was* something serious?
Willya A synchronous event.
Lazarus It sounded like a . . .
Brian It sounded pretty serious, Mr Ritsaat.
Mrs Hooley Yes, Mr Ritsaat.
Ritsaat (*draws gun from shoulder-holster*) Yeah. (*Exits up steps.*)

Bill Actually, we've collided with Uri Geller and he's tied a knot in the front half of the boat.

BILL pockets the 'ectoplasm'. CARSON returns.

Carson OK, session over – session over. Clements, you can get up now.

People drift towards the steps, looking first after RITSAAT, then back to CLEMENTS. BILL pulls CARSON to down right centre.

Bill Was that ectoplasm you got out of his stomach?

Carson Yeah.

Bill Would you just explain something to me? (*Produces 'ectoplasm' and examines it.*) It shows no sign of dissolving, and it's got something printed on it: 'Lever Brothers, Port Sunlight'. It's a soap wrapper.

Carson There was only one person that was meant to fool, which was Ritsaat.

Bill Oh, right. That's all right, then. For a moment you shook me. You couldn't do anything about my legs, could you?

Carson Nothing wrong with you, mate.

Glances towards CLEMENTS.

Did you know what this cunt is? A member of the CIA.

Bill Everyone talks to you, don't they?

Carson Even your daughter.

Bill She's not my natural daughter.

Carson I know. Clements fancies her.

Bill What should I do?

Carson Just thought I'd tell you.

Bill Thanks.

CARSON returns to CLEMENTS.

Carson Clements – wake up, you imperialist hyena.

Bill (*following*) Give him a popper. (*Produces one, hands it to CARSON.*)

Carson (*breaking popper under CLEMENTS's nose*) Personally, I never touch the stuff until five seconds before orgasm. Bad for the heart.

They watch.

Bill Not a tremor.

MARYLIN enters at top of steps in jeans and T-shirt, soaking wet.

Marylin Hi. I'm Marylin. You fuckers just ran over my boat.

General reaction.

Brian Oh, no! None of *us* was at the wheel.

Marylin That's it! Everybody I meet says it's not their fault. Christ, I'm surprised you even bothered to throw down a rope! What are you all on? Downers? (*Pause.*) What are you all doing down here?

Mrs Hooley Would you like a cup of tea? She's overwrought. (*Pours tea.*)

MARYLIN *comes down steps to left of the pyramid, sniffs, beats the air angrily.*

Marylin Oh, Christ! Who's on amyl nitrate? Or have you all just forgotten to change your socks?

Clements (*coming round*) I don't feel too good.

Carson Well, stay under the pyramid for a bit.

MRS HOOLEY *hands tea to* MARYLIN, *who sits left.*

Lazarus (*moving to her*) A disaster movie. There might be something in this. How many were killed?

Marylin No-one. Me and my girlfriend got picked up, but since we got on board I lost her. (*Takes tea from* MRS HOOLEY.)

WILLYA *exits down right.*

Lazarus What were you doing?

Marylin Sailing round the world. I was asleep. I need to find my friend.

RITSAAT *enters down the steps.* WILLYA *enters down right, carrying a towel.*

Lazarus (*sotto voce*) Here he comes – the spectre of world capitalism.

Ritsaat (*moves to* MARYLIN) Hi. My name's Ritsaat.

They shake hands.

Marylin What do *you* do?

Ritsaat Well, if this was Butlins, I'd be a Redcoat. (*Encourages all to laugh, then indicates* LAZARUS.) This man's hard work and imagination make it all possible. Clements? Carson, is he cured already?

Carson (*covering up*) He's just exhausted after the operation. The vibes . . . produced a fantastic synchronistic event – this lady and her friend.

Ritsaat Are you sure they're *ladies*?

Marylin Am I going to get compensation for my boat?

Ritsaat We'll talk about that in a minute, please. I hear you have a companion.

Marylin Yeah! I can't find her!

Ritsaat Just a moment. Stay right there. I'll look on the monitors. (*Exit down right.*)

Marylin What is he doing? Who *is* that guy?

Marks That's Mr Ritsaat.

Brian He's the boss around here. You'll have to talk to him.

CARSON *moves the bed to right.*

Marylin And he owns the ship, and you live down here?

Lazarus Well, it's all divided into compartments. (*Points.*) The bathroom's that way, there are some portable offices there, and we sleep in the dormitory over there.

Willya We used to go and play football on deck.

Marks But he's stopped that recently.

Wishbone Don't know why.

Mrs Hooley Because he wants us all to stay down here.

Lazarus I get so *bored*. You haven't brought any books, have you?

Marylin Why don't you stand up to him?

Lazarus That's what I ask everybody. I run around asking that question. He's just rather wearing to live with, and in the end you end up doing what he says.

A 'this is an announcement' bell, then RITSAAT's *voice is heard, with echo, on tape over the speaker system.*

Ritsaat (*tape*) She's nowhere! We must start the play immediately. OK, Lazarus – lick this bloody lot into shape. You can write, but you can't keep order. OK – show me!

Lazarus I mean – what can we do? It's his boat. OK – Cowboys to Beginners!

The 'Cowboys to Beginners' is, in effect, an 'Overture and Beginners' call to his performers, and a cluster begins to form upstage. WILLYA *hands the towel to* MARYLIN, *who dries her hair.*

Brian You must have had a terrible upset. Would you like an apple? (*Produces one from pocket, hands it to her.*)

Marylin Thanks. How did you all get to *be* here?

Willya There was this ad in the *Liverpool Echo*.

Mrs Hooley And *The Lady*. It was in *The Lady*.

Lazarus OK, fellers – get into line.

They do so.

Marylin What is going on?

Brian Same old thing: raising the whatsisname – the AntiChrist.

Mrs Hooley This time it's a play. You see, Brian and I used to work for Mr Ritsaat in Switzerland. It was lavish then. I don't know how Mr Ritsaat is going to make this one pay, though. We had guests then – we've no guests here now.

BILL *joins line.*

Brian You paid your money, and you were attacked. Attack by blizzard, attack by tornado, attack by Indians, attack by rather slow grizzly bears.

Mrs Hooley We were the bears.

Brian (*with a chuckle at the memory*) That was the worst part, y'know – having to burst in through the window, and make off with the pork chops – and I had sciatica. I used to run into the walls – I couldn't see where I was going.

Mrs Hooley They closed it down. They said there was a killing, and Mr Ritsaat was involved.

Brian We don't know that, Kathleen. All *we* know is that somebody got very badly attacked.

Lazarus Brian!

Brian Excuse me. (*Joins the line.*)

Mrs Hooley We've monitors, too, you know. Like they've got in supermarkets.

Marylin You're spied on the whole time?

Mrs Hooley Well, he just likes to keep an eye on us.

Marilyn Could we find my friend Sylvia on it?

Mrs Hooley I suppose so, but it's right up at the other end of the boat. (*With a gesture off down right.*)

Marylin (*rises*) Thanks. I must find her. (*Exits down right with towel.*)

Lazarus (*to down right*) All right! Now you're the labour monolith.

Marks What are we doing?

Lazarus Exactly what I tell you. If I say dance, you become dancers. If I say fart, then that's what you do.

Wishbone Oh, God!

Marks He's so vulgar.

Lazarus (*points front*) That's a cattle train. You're standing across the tracks, and you've got to frighten that driver into stopping. OK! (*Pause. Nothing from the line, so he stands down centre.*) Charge *me*! *I'm* a train! Stop me in my tracks!

They dribble up.

No, no . . . start again. Weak! Weak!

BRIAN *exits up left.* RITSAAT *enters down right and watches silently.*

Come back, BRIAN! We're short of people. We need everybody.

Brian Just a moment. Going to get an apple.

Ritsatt (*beckons*) Lazarus!

LAZARUS *breaks down right to him.*

What are you meant to be doing?

Lazarus I'm meant to be writing, not taking rehearsals.

Ritsaat Do they know remotely what they're meant to be doing? Don't you realise we might already have our visitor? So get a move on!

Lazarus (*piqued*) You want to take over?

Marks What are we doing?

Wishbone I've absolutely no idea what *I'm* doing.

Ritsaat Right. (*Hands jacket to* MRS HOOLEY *revealing shoulder holster.*) BRIAN! (*Exits up left.*)

MRS HOOLEY *exits up left with* RITSAAT'*s jacket.*

Marks ⎫
Wishbone ⎬ (*obediently*) BRIAN!
Lazarus ⎭

Bill (*down left, with* WILLYA) Seen anyone you fancy?

Willya No.

Bill Nobody you could love for half an hour? To support your poor crippled father in his old age?

Willya No.

Bill What about that dear man Clements?

Willya He's so old, he's practically a corpse.

Bill What d'you want? Always hanging around with Carson, the hippy.

Willya I want someone to play with my own age. (*Exits down right.*)

BRIAN *enters up left with box.* RITSAAT *follows him on.*

Ritsaat Brian, we're starting.

Brian I was just seeing if I could find an apple for the young lady.

Marks What's in the box?

Brian Nothing. One apple.

Ritsaat What's in the box, Brian?

Brian Otherwise air. Vapour. (*Rotten apples fall out of the box and spread over the floor.*) And one or two apples for my own personal consumption. *My* apples.

Ritsaat These are from the storeroom.

Brian I was keeping them in the storeroom, yes. You're very welcome, those of you who feel the need, to take one only. (*Gathers them.*)

Marks They're all mildewed. Is the box wet?

Brian Yes. That's why I was moving them to a safe, dry place.

Wishbone Ritsaat, it's perfectly clear to me that he's been pinching our food and hoarding it.

Ritsaat Look – can I look into that later, please? I don't want to have to legislate with petty squabbles amongst the crew.

Wishbone What are you trying to do to us, Brian? Are you deliberately blocking the Karzi, as well?

Brian There was a whole lot of cookers gone rotten with the damp. So I had to throw them away, and . . . as we're not allowed on deck because of the spy satellites . . . I thought I'd flush them down the toilet. I was only trying to be neat. I didn't know anyone wanted to use it. (*To* MRS HOOLEY.) I don't know what to do. There are *more* apples.

Marks Yours?

Brian Yes. (*Exits up left with box of apples.*)

Marks He's starting a black market in fruit!

Mrs Hooley No – he's too simple for that. It's just the taking he likes. (*Exits up left after* BRIAN.)

Ritsaat We've got to get on. Lazarus, how does it start?

Lazarus (*consulting his notes*) With the strike.

Ritsaat Who's going to *lead* the strike?

Lazarus Bill.

Bill Why me?

Ritsaat (*fast losing patience*) We are trying to scare up the AntiChrist, Bill! So how do you do that? You make solid what is usually shadowy and unreal. And in a strike, you see the labour monolith, shrouded in dreams of power, turning over in its sleep.

Bill Why don't we do the Russian revolution?

Ritsaat That would be courting disaster.

Marks Far too big a cast, luv.

Lazarus Shall I write the girls in?

Ritsaat Yes, definitely.

Wishbone It was an all-*male* society.

Marks Yes. Where did the girls come from, Mr Ritsaat?

Ritsaat It's a mystery, Marks. Carson is the expert on the unconscious.

Carson (*put on the spot*) Well, Rits. They might be aliens, or they might be Earth Spirits, come from the great sea of unconsciousness, out of which we are and to which we ultimately return . . .

Wishbone I still don't understand what the fuck we're doing!

Ritsaat Please be patient. Look, we carry spooled up inside us, the whole history of the human race. Cowboys are one of the primal states of Man.

BRIAN *and* MRS HOOLEY *enter up left.*

The native, the peasant – (*Indicates* BRIAN.) – the salt of the earth. Now, I want you to dig deep into yourselves, to find the racial memory. Lose yourselves for a moment. (*A pause, whilst they do so.*) Line up, hands on shoulders.

They form a line at the back of the stage.

Clements, do we have the pleasure of your company?

CLEMENTS *joins the end of the line, groggy.*

What was it like? Feel that mass behind you. Drum your heels. Harder! Harder! Now move down! That mighty colossus – defiance!

The line runs downstage with a yell, then instantly subsides.

Once more, with feeling! You see, Lazarus, that's how you should do it. Enthuse them. Even frighten them.

The line moves upstage.

This time you're going to be killed in the picket line! (*Draws his gun from its shoulder-holster.*) It's your last yell! Dig into yourselves – remember what it was like.

The line re-forms and charges down to RITSAAT, *yelling wildly. He fires his revolver into the air. They reach him. Blackout. Music for changeover.*

The pyramid is reset at centre. CLEMENTS *on it, in a coma, with his fur coat over him. The beer-crate is struck from beside the tea trolley, and the trolley is struck to off up right.*

SCENE 2

The same.

Two hours later, the same morning. The pyramid is centre-stage once more, with CLEMENTS *lying on it, in a coma, with his fur coat over him.*

Clements Mend the mirror of the past, restore the empty spaces. (*Pause.*) Endless, they seemed, the great plains.

WILLYA *enters up left removing a pair of doves, impaled together, from an arrow. She sits on the floor down right.*

The first time that men, as opposed to savages, had stood under that boundless sky . . . And they walked, to save the horses.

Distant jangling approaches from offstage up right.

The dishes in the wagon clacked endlessly, and I recall the irritation of the constant tinny jangle.

The jangling turns into MRS HOOLEY, *entering up right with her tea trolley. She moves with it to down right centre.*

Mrs Hooley Dear God! It's like miles, and when you get there, they've disappeared . . . (*To* WILLYA, *pouring milk.*) We were better off at Butlins. (*Hands her a mug of milk.*) We should have stayed at Butlins, you know, when we left Switzerland, but Brian was wrongfully accused of taking canteen cutlery, and we took our cards. (WILLYA *replaces mug.*) Mr Ritsaat understands temptation . . . Your granpa doesn't mean anything wrong. (*Exits left with trolley.*)

BILL *enters down left and moves to* WILLYA, *crouching at her side.*

Bill Did you get two pigeons with one arrow? Terrific.
Willya Not really – they were fucking.
Bill Fucking, were they? Listen – that fellow Carson, you know, he's no good for you. He's a hippy, that's what he is – a hippy. Now there's nothing wrong with Clements. Why don't you see if you can get him to give you that coat? Your mother used to do as much for me. She was a proper woman. Not some little chit with a bow and arrow. (*Crosses to left, waits for* WILLYA *to move, then exits down left.*)

WILLYA *steals up to* CLEMENTS *and lifts the coat from him.*

Clements (*sits on edge of bed, regaining consciousness briefly*) Willya –

WILLYA *drops the coat down right, then darts off down left.*

. . . there you are. Don't go. (*Loses consciousness again.*) Lady, who am I talking to? (*Another incarnation.*) My name is Myrna Grenville. I've told this tale a number of times. I ain't accustomed to lying. It was out west of Chicago, and we were on foot, and forced to the side of the track by a shooting. One big feller says, 'Draw.' The other says, 'Draw yourself.' 'I shall count to three,' says the first, egging him on.

SYLVIA *emerges up right, torn and wet. She sees the coat on the floor, and watches* CLEMENTS *in amazement.*

'Ain't I seen you before? Ain't you a troublemaker? Disruptin' property and molestin' women?' Something like that – I can't remember the exact words.

Sylvia (*moving to him*) Excuse me, love, is that your coat?

Clements And the big feller drawed when he hadn't counted past one. Shot him through the mouth, so he died . . . I was that glad to get through the plains, and settle down in California.

Sylvia (*pause*) Hello . . . I'm putting the coat on. Right?

Pause. She puts the coat on, taking her wet stuff off beneath it, her back to CLEMENTS. CLEMENTS *regains consciousness once more, watches her undressing for a few moments.*

Clements Can I turn round now? (SYLVIA *turns.*) Better hurry up, every time I pass out, you seem to age fifteen years. I'm not used to all these hallucinations. Most of the time I'm a fur trader. This guy Ritsaat's a joke on the Mission Impossible file. We gave him the money as a tax loss. Then they had to send me along. I'm a fur trader – that's my cover. Been married six times. The coat is wild Russian mink, with a platinum pinstripe lining. I had it made up in England: they've still got the best cutters. It's practically priceless. You know – you're beautiful. I wish I wasn't so cold. (*Towards her.*) Am I too old for love at first sight? The last time it happened was in Petrograd. I go there twice a year for the fur sales. I kept a mistress there for years. During the Siege she lost all her teeth. She sure was a dab hand at that there fellatio. (*Strokes her arm.*) Minks have got sharp teeth. Friend of mine had a mink ranch, and one day they were choosing pelts, wearing heavy gauntlets. One pesky little bastard bit him right through to the bone. 'Right!' he said. 'Pelt him! Pelt him!' And they took the skin off, just like that. By the way, my name's Clements. Fancy a little bourbon and some conversation in my cabin?

SYLVIA *begins to put her arms about his neck, as* WILLYA *enters down left, not noticing her.*

Willya Bill sent me back. He said I should charge two dollars for putting your coat on, if you were cold.

Clements (*handing money to her*) Here's five bucks, kid – now beat it!

Sylvia (*seeing her daughter*) WILLYA?!!
Willya Mummy!

   They embrace at centre.

Sylvia Oh, my baby! I knew I'd see you again!
Clements You two mother and daughter? (*Sotto voce.*) I don't believe it!
   That's just – well – *some*thing. Oh – gee – keep the fur coat.
Sylvia Who's looking after you? I'll look after you now. (*Pause.*) Is *he* here?
Willya Yes.
Sylvia Has he been interfering with you?
Willya I don't know.
Sylvia Has he?
Willya I'm all right. I'm fine.
Sylvia I bet the bastard got you on here so he could do it and not get pro-
   secuted. I bet you haven't got a school here. I bet there's no school.
Willya He's looking after me.
Sylvia That's what I'm afraid of. Girls of your age shouldn't have grown men
   to look after them. That's what happened to me.
Willya I know.
Bill (*off*) Hey! Hey! Hey! Who's saying rude words to my little daughter?
   (*Enters down left, moves to* WILLYA *at left centre.*) Oh . . . it's you.
Sylvia You abducted my daughter from me.
Bill That's not true. What are you doing here? Have we docked?
Sylvia You barred me from your parents' flat!
Bill *They* barred you! They thought you'd be taking customers in the front
   parlour.
Sylvia You poisoned their minds against me. You told them I was a whore.
   You never said anything about the Open University course, or how
   you'd forced me into giving it up, and being a full-time hooker for you
   with your precious legs. There's nothing bloody wrong with your legs!
Bill I went to Lourdes. I had polio. If God couldn't cure it, there must be
   something wrong with them.
Sylvia And I bet you've been persuading her to start on the game. If she's not
   too young for you, she won't be too young for others. And she'll do
   anything to prove I'm being too strict with her.

   MARKS *and* WISHBONE *enter up right as* RITSAAT's *'heavies'.*

Willya Look, it's a million million to one chance you met. Shouldn't you be
   pleased to see each other?
Sylvia (*speaks with* BILL) Shut up, or I'll shut you up!
Bill (*speaks with* SYLVIA) Shut up, you little twat!

   WILLYA *breaks to left centre, pockets the five-dollar bill.*

Marks Sylvia? You *must* be Sylvia. This is Wishbone, and I'm Marks. Would you have a word with our sponsor? He's sent us here to kidnap you at all costs, and bring you down to the blunt end of the boat.

Sylvia What for?

Bill That's Tweedledum and Tweedledee. They're not there, really.

Wishbone We are simply carrying out Mr Ritsaat's wishes, his request, OK?

Bill Go on, then. He might be offering you a part in a blue movie.

Sylvia Who are they?

Bill They're harmless.

Marks Sylvia, would you like to take an arm?

Sylvia I'll return the coat later.

> MARKS *and* WISHBONE *take* SYLVIA *off down right.* CARSON *enters up right.*

Carson The speakers have gone. Totalled. BAM! My life savings. (*Moves down to right centre.*)

Bill That was because you interfered with Clements, wasn't it?

Carson Oh, was that it?

> WILLYA *crosses to* CARSON, *who puts an arm round her.*

Bill Rushing him back to the Wild West without telling him. *I'm* not ready, and I've been practising me draw for years. Isn't that right, Clements?

Clements I dunno, I got one hell of a hangover from somewhere. I didn't have it when I woke up this morning. I must have still been drunk. (*Puts a hand lightly on* BILL's *shoulder.*)

> BILL *jumps away.* CLEMENTS *does likewise.*

Hey, sorry about that. It's static.

Bill How d'you build up static in your body, when the rest of us don't?

Clements Oh, it's a life spent running up and down nylon carpets in whore-houses.

Bill (*produces a pack of cards*) D'you want to lose your shirt?

Clements I already lost my coat. Yeah, all right. (*Breaks down left.*)

> CARSON *and* WILLYA *are looking up at the pyramid.* BILL *sees them.*

Bill Pyramids didn't save the Pharoahs. I don't know why you bother with them.

Carson Well, it's the shape, innit.

Bill You can't make a perfect copy of anything in this world.

Carson Why not?

Bill Well, it's all down to Eisenberg's Uncertainty Principle. Quantum Physics, which deals with the finite amounts of energy possibly present in matter, drives a horse and cart through any possibility of real dup- lication in this world, wouldn't you say?

Carson (*pause*) I accept the argument, but this is a model – a perfectly reduced shape. Course, it's not as big.

Bill Yes, and the original is outside in the weather, isn't it? Expanding in the sun and shrinking at night. It must be up and down like a milkman. How d'you get to measure that?

Carson (*pause*) Well, the original idea of the Uncertainty Principle comes from a rather flawed crucible, too. Eisenberg's a Nazi protegé. The pyramid's a *demonstration* of an ideal shape. Any pyramid's an approximation to it, including the original. Platonic idea.

Bill How can you have a straight line, when it's something men carry round in their heads?

Carson Approximation.

Bill Space and time are curved.

Carson I know.

Bill Space and time are curved!

Carson And one of them's got a nasty cough, too.

Bill You read your Einstein, mate. Teach yourself something for a change. (*Turns.*) Come on, Clements. (*Flicks the cards.*) You haven't got a chance.

BILL *and* CLEMENTS *exit down left.*

WILLYA *picks up white crystals from where* CLEMENTS *has been lying.*

Willya Snow! Does that mean we're time-travelling? (*Sits under pyramid.*)

Carson (*sits left of her*) I dunno about you – but I'd love to go back to eighteen eighty-six. Think of the money you could make, inventing diodes, semi-conductors and transistors. You'd be so fucking rich . . .

Willya And if I came with you, there wouldn't be any problems with your wife? . . .

Carson Quite. As it is, as soon as she finds out anything on the side, she tends to pour meths into the hi-fi and set a torch to it. That's what she did last time. She's a wise woman. She's not like you. You're beautiful – she's very ugly. But she knows where my heart is. It's in electronics. (*Pause.*) And the problem is that I got convictions for the possession of the dreaded ganja weed, so I keep getting planning permission for a recording studio turned down.

Willya What's ganja weed?

Carson Oh, it's . . . like the sixties, it's before your time. We're all too old for you, Willya.

Willya Yes – you are a bit *old*, aren't you?

Carson Don't say it like *that*.

Willya And a bit clapped-out, too. I thought you were *some*thing . . . I thought you were my friend. But you're not. You're just like the others – dead ordinary. (*Collects bow and arrow from down right.*)

SCENE 3

RITSAAT's *office.*

Lights. RITSAAT, *with a rubber-covered torch, leads* SYLVIA *on from up left.*

He switches on lights, puts down the torch, then sits SYLVIA *in the swivel-chair at down left centre.*

Ritsaat Sit down, please. I want to have a look at you. That's a good pair of legs. Do they go all the way up?

SYLVIA *moves to lift her skirt.*

No, you don't have to show me! Would you like a cup of tea? There's a machine. (*Moves towards it.*) Nesquik, coffee – takes washers. Here.

Sylvia No, thanks.

Ritsaat I suppose I should say 'welcome aboard'. But first . . . there are things to clear up. I've been working in the field of politico-psychic research for some years now. I had a research station in Switzerland where some really weird things happened.

SYLVIA *tries to comment.*

Don't speak. A postman, bearing a poison-pen letter for me, walked up to my door and burst into flames. So I'm not too easily surprised. Given that we are by choice in a psychically unstable part of the world, I need some confirmation that you are who you say you are: Bill's common-law wife Sylvia. I'm going to put it to you straight. Are you human?

Sylvia What's human?

Ritsaat Someone who has free choice.

Sylvia Count me out, then.

Ritsaat Someone who isn't harbouring the AntiChrist, for instance. You're not harbouring the AntiChrist, are you?

Sylvia I've got a rash.

Ritsaat Can I see it? (*Pause.*) All right. (*Indicates portrait, a huge photo of* RITSAAT *in uniform dwarfing all else.*) Does that do anything for you?

Sylvia It's good.

Ritsaat In what sense is it good?

Sylvia It's a good photo.

Ritsaat Go on. For what reason?

Sylvia It's a good photo . . . because the eyes follow you round the room.

Ritsaat That was in my political days. But I realised that the black tide was going to wipe my country off the map, however we dressed up the final solution, so I changed tactics. (*Pause.*) Do you believe in coincidence? If so, isn't it, an amazing coincidence to collide with the ship that has your father-in-law, your mother-in-law, your husband and your daughter on it? It does stretch the old credibility a bit, doesn't it? All right.

(*Collects file from drawer of cabinet, looks through it, is surprised by what he finds.*) Bill tells me you're on the game.

Sylvia I didn't have much choice. I was sweeping the roads, doing a course at the Open University. And because I had Willya with me all the time, I got the sack. They said it was because I drank at lunch. Then I came back with this bloke one night, and found Bill fiddling with Willya on the couch. It's what happened to me – *my* father . . . I know Bill's not *her* father, but I swore it wouldn't happen to my kid, and it did. Can I ask you a favour?

Ritsaat Ask me anything.

Sylvia (*rise to centre*) I want my child looked after properly. I don't want her molested.

Ritsaat That's every mother's right.

Sylvia Will you see that it's done?

Ritsaat Yeah. Now, what we'll do – (*Goes to filing-cabinet, leaves file, produces drug bottles.*) – is give you sodium pentathol, LSD, adrenalin to accelerate the acid trigger, seconal to balance the adrenalin; and then in this 'light trance' you'll tell us everything you know about you, yourself, rashes, tattoos – the works. With your permission.

Sylvia Are you different afterwards?

Ritsaat Could be. Confession changes some people. What have *you* got to confess? (*A new idea.*) Have you had ECT?

Sylvia Therapy? No – I'd like that. Is it good for you?

Ritsaat (*puts drugs away, produces wires and box – all in one deft sweep*) We've got the stuff here.

Sylvia I do get pains.

Ritsaat Pains?

Sylvia Yeah. Can I have the treatment and go?

Ritsaat I'll have to treat you. Ship's doctor is busy with another case.

Sylvia (*takes wires from him*) I'll do that. I'll go behind here – I don't want you to watch. (*Goes behind coffee dispenser.*)

Ritsaat Moisten the pads and put them on your temples.

Sylvia (*pause*) I've done that. Are you watching?

Ritsaat No. Ready?

Sylvia Not yet.

RITSAAT *turns on the current.* SYLVIA *screams and screams, reaching above the dispenser for a cup of Nesquik.* MARYLIN *rushes in up left, tears the leads out of the box.*

Ritsaat What's this? What are you doing? (*Grabs her.*)

They struggle. SYLVIA *emerges, naked, trance-like, but not without seeing* MARYLIN.

Sylvia I loved an Indian. His name was . . .

Ritsaat (*turns, sees naked flesh, turns away again*) Oh, sorry.

SYLVIA *'comes to', collects her coat from behind the dispenser and puts it back on.*

Marylin You *monster*!

Ritsaat I was just getting her more receptive.

Marylin She's got wires up her fanny, covered in her own excrement, and you're improving her *mind*?

Sylvia It's all right. I'm all right.

Ritsaat She wanted that. *She* put them there. *I* told her her head. Why did you do that, Sylvia?

Sylvia I wanted it. All right? I can look after myself, now. (*Moves left, sits in the swivel chair.*)

Marylin You can't just do that to people.

Ritsaat She consented. Don't you ever knock?

Marylin What about the dignity of the human race?

Ritsaat Personally, I'm for it. (*Looks at monitors.*)

Marylin (*moving to* SYLVIA) I lost you!

Ritsaat (*fiddling with controls*) Now where's everybody gone? Excuse me. I look after a number of people. . . . It's important for me to see where they went. I criticise them when they go wrong, but they can't all have left me, can they?

Marylin Sylvia, why do you do this to me?

Ritsaat Excuse me. They must be on deck. They're not allowed on deck. They can't do this to me. (*Rushes out up left.*)

Marylin (*moves to* SYLVIA) Sylvia, I've been looking for you for two hours. You must have known you were lost. Why do you do this to me? Ten minutes more, and he would have been carving you up!

Sylvia You know what started him off? All my family are on board.

Marylin I think I met them.

Sylvia Will you try and get on with them?

Marylin OK.

Sylvia Don't cause trouble.

Blackout. The portrait and monitors are flown out, and the shower flown in. The dispenser, cabinet, chair and props are struck, and two benches are set. A steam valve is set left of the shower unit.

SCENE 4

The shower-room. A huge pipe. Small, cramped. One portable, plastic shower, curtained. Dirty place, walls of canvas. Steam everywhere. MARKS *is discovered sitting on the bench at left facing front.* WISHBONE *is standing at centre. Both in towels.*

Marks 'You're looking very lovely, you know, in this damned moonlight. Your skin is clear and cool, and your eyes are shining, and you're growing lovelier and lovelier every second as I look at you. You don't hold any mystery for me, darling, do you mind? There isn't a particle of you that I don't know, remember and want.'

Wishbone 'I'm glad, my sweet.'

Marks 'More than any desire anywhere, deep down in my deepest heart I want you back again . . . please – '

Wishbone 'Don't say any more, you're making me cry so dreadfully.' (*Change of mood.*) Isn't it, 'You're looking damnably attractive in that *damnable* moonlight?'

Marks No it isn't! I have done it many times.

Wishbone Of course you have. I was forgetting.

Marks (*pause, sits on right bench*) If this is time-travel, I'd rather be doing a matinée of *The Comedy of Errors* at Wimbledon – to the Fire Officer in January.

Wishbone (*pause*) What's the most boring Shakespearian comic part you've ever played.

Marks (*pause*) Young Gobbo. Followed by Old Gobbo. (*They laugh.*)

Wishbone (*with a chuckle*) Old Gobbo is really the pits, isn't he?

Marks Yes . . .

LAZARUS *enters centre, from right. Sits up stage end of left bench, towelled.*

Wishbone (*sharp*) Just before anyone else comes in, have you written anything yet? (*Pause.*) You're just waiting, still. What are you waiting *for*?

Marks You've heard of leading screenwriters, Wishbone? Well, Lazarus is a *trailing* one.

Wishbone But we've got to start soon. I'm not bloody signing on for *another* six months. Quick, man!

Marks Are we not going to do it?

Wishbone I'm still an aristocrat, am I?

Lazarus (*sarcastically*) You're as aristocratic as you ever were.

WILLYA *and* BILL *enter centre, from right, towelled.*

Marks How are you getting on with him? Still get the legs chopped off?

Lazarus (*nods*) Mm-hmm.

Bill That's fine. Just so long as it's not cinema verité.

BILL *and* WILLYA *sit downstage of* LAZARUS, *with* WILLYA *between them and a space between her and* LAZARUS. CARSON *helps* CLEMENTS *on at centre, from right, sits him on the steam vent.* CLEMENTS *appears heavily frosted.*

Wishbone Look, Carson, what have you done? Carved a model of Clements out of ice-cream?

Marks He's not well, you know.

Carson I don't know what's wrong with him. He's probably been wired up by the CIA for instant cryogenics, and by mistake has bitten on the fatal tooth. He'll probably wake up fresh as a daisy in the middle of the twenty-first century.

Marks Why is he sitting on the steam valve?

Clements (*fierce*) Because I'm *cold*.

Carson There's nothing really wrong with him. By the way, who smashed up my pyramid? I took a lot of time and trouble to get the measurements right, and now someone's taken a wrecking-bar to it. Was it either of you two?

Wishbone Look, love, it's not really our scene: football hooliganism, and so forth. Have you asked the Irish contingent?

Marks Yes, it sounds like the paddy factor. Mindless destruction.

> MARYLIN *enters centre, from right, sits at downstage end of right bench.* CARSON *stands at upstage end of same bench.*

Marylin Excuse me.

Bill (*pause*) That fella's a hooey.

Wishbone Who?

Bill Carson. That stuff this morning was faked. Chartres has Mary's veil: I have Carson's polythene. (*Produces 'plasma'.*)

Wishbone Really? Frightful, if it was. I mean – I don't know, he did wonders for my fibrositis. Just waved his jewelled fingers over my rump.

Bill And sealed up your arse forever.

> SYLVIA *enters centre, from right. She sees* WILLYA, *sits upstage of* BILL.

Marylin I'm over here, Sylvia.

> SYLVIA *sits in* MARYLIN'*s place.* MARYLIN *stands behind her.*

Bill Don't mind us – we're married.

Willya Mummy, where have you been?

Bill On her back, most likely.

Sylvia Shut up, Bill.

> MRS HOOLEY *and* BRIAN *enter centre, from right, fully dressed, and sit on the left bench, with* BRIAN *at upstage end.* LAZARUS *rises to make room for them.*

Mrs Hooley Does he mind us all mixed up in here?

Carson Don't worry about it, Mrs Hooley. The microphone's rusted, and the TV lens has steamed up.

Lazarus Mrs Hooley: we are many, and he is one.

Mrs Hooley But he could come in, and he's been very good to Brian and myself.

Brian He won't come in here.

Mrs Hooley He might, and I don't want to offend anyone. We've worked for Mr Ritsaat for ever such a long time, back in Switzerland. (*Glances* *towards* BILL.) Hasn't Bill lost a lot of weight, Brian?

Lazarus Mrs Hooley, we *are* having a meeting!

Marylin Who's chairing it?

LAZARUS *attempts to rise.*

Marks (*rising*) I will.

LAZARUS *sits.*

Wishbone Mister Chairman.

Marks You have the floor. (*Sits.*)

Wishbone (*rises*) I move a motion of censure against Lazarus for failing repeatedly to produce a script for inspection. I don't believe he's written anything, let alone a part for me as an English aristocrat.

Carson (*rises*) Who needs a script?

Marks (*rises*) Through the chair, please.

Carson Plays often don't have scripts.

Lazarus (*rises*) Are you trying to get rid of me?

Carson Look, we should be able to produce something out of the collective unconscious.

Reaction. MARKS *and* WISHBONE *sit.*

I'm only suggesting it in desperation, because 'Laz' isn't up to writing a script.

Lazarus Try me!

Marks Everybody has, love.

Lazarus OK. Fine. I quit. (*Sits.*)

Marylin Could you satisfy my curiosity? I don't know if it's my place to say this, but I don't know why you're working for Ritsaat at all.

Carson Yeah – and does anyone know who smashed up my pyramid?

Bill It was Willya.

Pause.

Mrs Hooley (*pause*) Pooh, it's hot, isn't it, Brian?

Lazarus You are free to leave at any time, Mrs Hooley.

Brian I think I might take my trousers off, if Kathleen doesn't mind. (*Removes boiler-suit.*)

CARSON *sits.*

Marylin What is it exactly? Are you trying to find out by consensus if Ritsaat is mad?

Brian He's not mad.

Sylvia He's mad, all right.

Mrs Hooley Mr Ritsaat is not mad. You watch your tongue.

Marylin Tell them, Sylvia. Come on, honey – don't be afraid. Just tell them exactly what he did to you.

Sylvia Well, I got dragged off to see him, and he took me off through the dark into this funny room, and showed me this photo of him all dressed up in uniform. So I thought – 'Oh-Oh.' And he was very proud of it, and kept asking me what I liked about it. So I thought there was some funny business coming up. He gave me these two electrodes, and wanted to give me ECT. I said OK, thinking he wants to knock me out and, you know, have it with me. So I didn't fancy that at all, so I went behind the coffee machine and laid the two pads on the floor – and they started to spark! So I had to think of something to put him off, so I grabbed a cup of Nesquik and poured it over my crutch to pretend I'd gone to the toilet. And then Marylin came in, and he stopped, so I said the first thing that came into my head.

Lazarus What was that?

Sylvia Something about being in love with an Indian.

Lazarus Good move. I'll work it in.

Sylvia And then I left.

Lazarus Terrific, Sylvia – terrific.

Sylvia It could have been very nasty.

Marylin If this guy is mad, pathologically, there's no way you should be working for him.

Bill We've only Sylvia's word for it.

Brian He's not mad. He's strict.

Mrs Hooley He's been good to us.

Bill He's got some funny ideas.

Sylvia He's *mad*, Bill.

Mrs Hooley Would you take the word of a common streetwalker against a gentleman?

Willya Mummy, what happened? Nobody's telling the truth!

Mrs Hooley (*rises*) She wouldn't know the truth if she saw it. She's nothing but a whore!

Uproar, general.

Sylvia (*rising*) You lot have always conspired against me!

Marylin (*rising*) Now listen, there are things you could work for which would make it a lot easier here. Have you thought of going on strike?

Silent reaction. SYLVIA *sits.*

Mrs Hooley (*pause*) We couldn't do that. We'd never get paid.

Brian On strike? Over what?

Marylin Lousy food, bad accommodation, what looks like dangerous working conditions. Have you thought of getting the monitors turned off?

Carson What – at night, in the dormitories?

Marylin No. Turned off – period.

An excited buzz.

Who's preparing a list of demands?
Bill (*pause*) I will.

LAZARUS *hands him pen and paper. He writes.*

Lazarus Number one – better food. That's for Mrs Hooley.
Carson Fat chance.
Wishbone Number two – better accommodation. D'you know, except for
    Clements, we're all in the same room in bunks?
Lazarus Number three?
Marylin Number three – no monitors.
Marks No monitors in the dormitories . . .
Marylin No monitors *ever!*
Carson Number four – we ought to be allowed on deck, out of working hours.
All Yes!
Willya And we should be allowed to talk to the crew again.
Marylin Number six – –

RITSAAT *enters centre, from right. All scramble for saftey, silence falls.*

Ritsaat (*pause*) So, it's a conspiracy! I knew it! (*To* MARYLIN.) You put them
    up to this, I suppose.
Marylin No, Ritsaat. It's a completely spontaneous movement of the masses
    towards freedom.
Ritsaat Let's have a look. (*Takes list from* BILL, *reads.*) 'Better food. Better
    accommodation. No monitors, ever. Permission to go on deck at any
    time.' (*Pause.*) Better food. I couldn't agree more. Mrs Hooley – either
    you learn to cook, or we'll cook you. (*He encourages them to laugh.*)
    Accommodation. Marks, I suggest you get up a working party, and
    divide the dormitory into single accommodation. OK? And no monitors.
    Yes, they are a mistake, twenty-four hours a day. We'll just have them
    during playing time. Fine. Yes. OK? Is Clements OK, Carson?
Carson He's fine. Just a bit of post-operative shock. He'll come out of it in no
    time.
Ritsaat I trust you. Lazarus, how's the writing doing?
Lazarus I got a block.
Ritsaat Is that my fault? You eat too much. You should keep trim like me.
    (*Opens shirt.*) Look, look. (*Tucks it in.*) So. We go ahead. Ja?

General reaction of agreement.

I'm going to turn the monitors off now. And then I'm going up on
deck. Anyone coming to taste the night air?

MARKS *and* WISHBONE *stand*

It's quite cold out.
Wishbone Which way are we heading?

Ritsaat Now: tomorrow, we'll be in the middle of the Bermuda Triangle. If we're quick. The sooner we get there, the sooner we start.

Blackout. Spot on RITSAAT. *From Rod Stewart's 'Sailing', briefly.*

In blackout, fly out shower unit and backing, strike the benches, rostrum and steam vent. Fly in star cloth upstage, set ship's rail down left centre.

SCENE 5

On deck. Deck rail with battered life belt, inscribed indistinctly 'Myrna Grenville'.

Wind machine and stars on. Sea and engine noises. Melt the spot to a low, wider light. RITSAAT *is discovered at the rail, lighting a cigar with a cigarette-lighter. Pause.*

MARYLIN *enters from up left, wearing the fur coat, and joins him. Pause. They look front.* MARYLIN *points to side.*

Marylin (*pause*) What's that over there? Those lights? Anything to do with you?

Ritsaat Probably the Cubans having a fireworks party for Castro.

Marylin I read about the CIA planning to fake the Second Coming, so they could grab Cuba back.

Ritsaat (*pause*) I got some money from the CIA for this. They think I'm rich, but I'm not. I'm the black sheep. My brother – he's making all the money. I hired this ship on pluck and bluff. I'm a cheeky chappie, so I get things done.

Marylin Why did you fill it up with gays?

Ritsaat It was a complete mistake. The ad never mentioned sex. It was about 'cowboy fun'. I know I'm right in other group characteristics.

Marylin How do you mean?

Ritsaat They're generally of middle to low intelligence; easily suggestible – something about the eyes; very few of them have any leadership potential. That's why, when you came along, you find yourself in this supersaturated solution of complaints. A leader appears, and – click! The situation suddenly crystallises. Are you going to lead them in revolt against me?

Marylin First they have to ask me.

Ritsaat Oh, no! A leader and a democrat! Very good. I like you. I like you a lot. Your friend is the focus of some friendly attention, isn't she?

Marylin It always happens to her.

Ritsaat So you took her to sea to escape. And here we are, all going to sea for the opposite reason, and – nothing. Neither of us seems to be very good at planning our lives, do we? She'll go back with Bill, now. He's . . . been having her daughter. He can't keep his hands off her. It's disgusting, but what can you do? Castration?

Marylin What are you looking for?

Ritsaat What I'm looking for is the real reason behind history. History we're taught at schools is about a random succession of imperial events. History we learn after we leave is about a random succession of plagues, wars and poverties. Neither theory explains everything. Even you radicals know that there are reasons *behind* the reasons of history. I believe the AntiChrist is behind it all.

Marylin Do they believe that? (*Pause.*) Why did they come with you, if they knew they were going to be so ill-treated?

Ritsaat Ignorance and poverty. The usual first causes of movement – ignorance and poverty.

BRIAN, BILL, MRS HOOLEY, SYLVIA *and* WILLYA *are heard from offstage, drunk, singing 'In Our Liverpool Home'.*

See? Too many of them from one family. Perhaps he wants them with me . . . I don't know. Maybe they're not a plant. Maybe *you're* a plant . . . No – I'm not going to give Lazarus or anyone any more clues.

The merrymakers are heard greeting the crew: 'Hey! Amigos!'

(*Points off left.*) Look at that lot – talking to the crew. I discovered that three of the crew are Cubans. They say they left before the Revolution. What kind of friends do you think they had, if they knew it was coming?

Marylin I think you've been at sea too long.

Ritsaat So – what are you going to do? If you want to leave, I'll give you the money to get back. It's against the spirit of what I'm doing to have you here. But I am learning a kind of surrender to events: they have their own logic. You must make up your own mind: to stay and work with Lazarus, or to go home on your own. You're too smart, really, to stay. But then – 'If you are noble, then I will love you' – Whitman.

Marylin Sylvia won't leave now.

Ritsaat No, she won't. She was *your* girl, eh? That's too bad. You're going to have to hide your love away.

Marylin Charades or isolation – the social dilemma. I'll stay.

Ritsaat Right – I'm going in now. There's a new Russian satellite rising in ten minutes. They mustn't see me.

Marylin Can I ask a simple question?

Ritsaat Make it quick.

Marylin What has the Cowboy Strike to do with the AntiChrist?

Ritsaat Do you really think that Marxist Jewish Hollywood gave us the truth? The truth is that most people in the West died of a bullet in the *back* of the head – that's if they managed to survive maiming and blood-poisoning. The first building in a plains town was a brothel, set in a tent, behind a clap-board façade. Drunk men in waistcoats and bowler hats, and foetid women. Christ? You can smell it, can't you? I've seen it – those desperate men, those broken women in immigrant clothes.

Hatred and fear from dead eyes. A moral vacuum to suck in the Anti-Christ! (*Becomes increasingly Hitlerian, volume rising to crescendo.*) In the nineteenth century, the AntiChrist put on the garment of Communism, when it was the brainchild of Liberalism. He has now twisted it into totalitarianism so monstrous, that it threatens to destroy us all! He has rewritten the history books to confound us! Now, before his puppet Marx, he made the people run through fire for him! (*Pause.*) They keep asking, 'When will he come? When will he come?' Don't worry – if we get close enough, he'll come. Already something has started killing the doves. This can only mean one thing. (*Exits down right.*)

MARYLIN *looks after him, momentarily dumbfounded.*

Marylin (*pause*) Christ! (*Pause: look front.*) I am captive aboard an occult millenial death-factory. Why me? I mean – why *me*? (*Pause.*) Well, Marylin – it's probably God's way of saying He takes a rather dim view of what turns you on. Why don't you just write to your mother, and tell her you're going to go straight. And there's a good chance He'll treat you just like any other decent, ordinary Jew.

Pause. Blackout. Housetabs in. Music.

Strike ship's rail, fly out star cloth.

Preset train piece up right, masking curtains for same, a roll of lino with painted rail tracks, two beer-crates under the bench left, and a wind machine up left.

END OF ACT I

ACT II

SCENE 1

A week or two later. LAZARUS'*s play.*

There are two large beer-crates under the bench left, and third at up right. In the up right corner, a hand-operated wind machine. RITSAAT *is seated in the down right corner, on one of the folding canvas chairs, viewing* LAZARUS'*s play. The company are upstage.* LAZARUS *operates the wind machine as a pool of light builds at centre.* BRIAN *and* MRS HOOLEY *move downstage into the light. Full immigrant Irish rig, dirty faces and bowler hats. Key-rings with plates, knives and spoons on their belts. The actors are dressed more like the immigrant/ cowboy.* RITSAAT *remains the same.*

Brian (*pause*) The great plains.
Mrs Hooley The great plains.
Brian (*pause*) Have taken our only son. Dear God. I'm hungry.
Mrs Hooley God will provide.

They kneel and pray. At rear, the company, as COWBOYS, *make a 'herd of cattle' noise.* BRIAN *looks off down right.*

Brian Look, Kathleen! A whole herd of animals! Coming towards us!
Mrs Hooley He's done it again! God's done it again!

They exit down right. The 'cattle' noise continues.

(*Off*) I got one!
Brian (*off*) Kill it, quick!
Mrs Hooley (*off*) It's struggling!
Brian (*off*) Kick it in the balls!
Mrs Hooley (*off*) It's a cow, Brian!
Brian (*off*) Kick it in the cunt, then!

The 'cattle' noise dies. BRIAN *and* MRS HOOLEY *re-enter down right, each carrying a big piece of cold, cooked beef. They sit at centre and begin to eat.* CLEMENTS *appears, as Sheriff, from up left.* BRIAN *sees him, nudges* MRS HOOLEY.

Look, Kathleen. Who's that man over there with a star on his chest?
Mrs Hooley (*rising*) Look . . . we found it, lying there. . . .

The line of COWBOYS, *dimly top-lit, stomps in rhythm, a huge butch chorus line. They charge downstage, yelling wildly.* BRIAN *and* MRS HOOLEY *disappear behind them, and exit upright.* COWBOYS *split up and become a confused rabble.* CLEMENTS *breaks through them.*

Clements Boys, what in the hell is going on here? There's cattle running wild out there . . . tearing themselves to pieces on the barbed-wire. (*Pause.*) Someone answer me! I've a hanging party to make up. Any takers?

Carson Anyone we know?

Clements Couple of Irish stole a steer. Course, if you boys weren't on strike, there wouldn't be loose cows running around. Whose idea is this, blocking the train?

Lazarus No, sir. It ain't my idea.

Carson (*pointing to* BILL) Belongs to him.

Clements Who?

Marks (*pointing*) Him.

The COWBOYS *back off to leave* BILL *at* CLEMENTS'*s mercy.*

Clements Ain't seen you before.

Bill I bin working the Sedalia trail.

Clements What you doing up here, then?

Bill Living peaceably in my habitation.

Clements (*leading* BILL *downstage*) I know this bunch, and they ain't got enough brains between 'em to make soup! What you gone and made 'em do.

Bill Well . . . We haven't been paid – for months. We thought we might – sit down in front of the train.

Clements It ain't your train.

Bill It takes our cows.

Clements It ain't your train!

Bill That's the truth, now.

CLEMENTS *draws a .45 from the hip, and mimes firing his gun at the cowboys' feet, with* LAZARUS *producing the shots from a starting pistol.* COWBOYS *exit.*

Clements (*holsters his gun, with much show*) That's better. We don't take kindly to troublemakers. Say, you ain't by chance one of those anarchist communist agitators?

Bill (*in big trouble*) No, no, no, no, none of those.

Clements You seem a bright young fellow. I'm looking for a new deputy – but one of the requirements is that you have to live here in the county. Where exactly is your peaceable habitation?

Bill Two miles west, out of town. You take a right, and another right. . . .

Clements Don't fuss yourself. I'll find it. Say, where did you get that dumb idea of sitting on the tracks?

Ritsaat (*interrupting the play*) Hold it right there! (*Rises.*)

Now that the play has been stopped, the company wander back onstage slowly, and CLEMENTS *exits left.*

Did anyone else hear that? That noise? Wait! It came from above us. That didn't sound like a collision. Or did it?

WILLYA *enters up left.*

Bill (*sarcastically*) It sounded like icebergs.

Ritsaat Break it there, will you? (*Runs off up steps.*)

Lazarus (*centre*) If he keeps on jumping in like this, we'll never get home. I'm three weeks ahead of him already. (*Turns* RITSAAT'*s chair to front, sits, writes furiously in notebook.*)

MARKS *and* WISHBONE *exit up right, returning with a table and a bentwood chair which they set down centre. On the table, a pan of navy beans and a piece of hoof.* WISHBONE *then sets one of the crates from under the bench left at left centre for* CLEMENTS.

Willya (*moving to* LAZARUS) Granma says she'll pluck the pigeons for . . .

Lazarus Ace. A-one. I'll cook them. We can have them together, just you and me – chocolate sauce. That way she can't burn them.

Willya But I can't find anymore.

Lazarus You must have shot them all. Willya, can you leave me alone? I'm hitting gold.

Willya What is it?

Lazarus It's a speech for the AntiChrist. It lasts about another half an hour. It's a dynamite speech.

Willya But there's no-one to say it.

Lazarus Willya, one day you may grow up and see the original version of *The Big Sleep*, and afterwards you may wonder who shot the chauffeur. The answer is that no-one shot him. In fact, the script came in and shot him – and – bam! He was *dead*! That's how versatile scripts are. Forget actors, forget directors, forget dialogue coaches –

Willya What are they?

Lazarus In the beginning was the *word*. (*Returns to writing.*)

Carson (*approaching* LAZARUS) I thought only Ron Hubbard wrote that fast.

Willya We haven't got anyone to play the AntiChrist. Lazarus is writing a speech for him.

Carson (*miffed*) He's a mite previous, isn't he? I can do astral projection, transmigration of souls – bodies are something else. And if he doesn't materialise soon, we're going to have to go and get him.

MARYLIN *enters up left, marches up to* BILL, *turns him by the shoulder to face her.*

Marylin Here, this is for you, you pimp. (*Hits him full on the jaw.*)

BILL *stands there, reeling.* BRIAN *and* MRS HOOLEY *run on from up right to protect him.*

You bastard!

Mrs Hooley Don't you ever use that word on my son.

Marylin Bastard! Pimp! Ponce! Bastard!

Mrs Hooley You bold girl! Striking a poor disabled cripple!

Marylin He got his legs broken for pimping outside the wrong dance halls and that's all!

Mrs Hooley They was illset when he came to us.

Bill (*to* MRS HOOLEY) Shut up, will you!

Brian Leave it, Mother. He wants to stand on his own.

Mrs Hooley He needs people to look after him.

Bill I can look after myself.

Marylin Come on then, you working-class hero. Step outside.

> BILL *makes as though to pass her, then punches her hard in the stomach.* MARYLIN *is winded, but no-one goes to her aid.* BILL, BRIAN *and* MRS HOOLEY *exit up left with many a backward look.* CARSON *then moves gingerly to the injured* MARYLIN.

Carson Marylin, we were all behind you in spirit. Has he hurt you? (*Sits her at table centre.*)

> LAZARUS *sits on bench right, continues writing.*

Marylin I never thought I'd be pleased to be wearing whalebone stays.

Wishbone At last, somebody's standing up to the Hooleys.

Marks Not before time.

Carson You still having problems with your beloved?

Marylin I came in the shower, and she was being humped by Clements. Or that's what it looked like. I know you all want to get paid, and I'll keep my mouth shut about labour conditions – but not at the price of my girl being hooked up again. What the fuck am I doing, going along with all this?

Carson Love.

Marylin (*pause*) I thought I'd settled for lust.

> CLEMENTS *drifts up left, laughing.*

Clements Bill looks like he done run into Jack Dempsey!

Marylin (*rises*) Will you leave my girl alone?

Clements What?

Marylin Will you leave Sylvia alone?

Clements But . . . what?

Marylin She's my girl.

Clements No she ain't. She's Bill's girl, ain't she?

Marylin (*to* CARSON) I suppose the CIA send him on these Mickey Mouse missions to get him out from under their feet. Who are you, anyway?

Clements I can't disclose my rank to you.

Marylin Who killed Kennedy?

> MARKS *and* WISHBONE *back off, left.* CARSON *joins* LAZARUS *at right.*

Clements *I* know who killed Kennedy.

Marylin Donald Duck?

Clements You'd last about ten minutes in the Warsaw countries, before you would be sent off to be re-educated.

Marylin What is the CIA doing here?

Clements (*pause and glance at* MARKS *and* WISHBONE) We have a commitment to match the investment into parapsychological warfare of the other side.

Marylin Crap!

Clements And we've decided not to abort, even though we are harbouring a sexual and political deviant.

Marylin What are you talking about?

Clements I got your file out of the computer.

SYLVIA *enters up left, doing up her dress, and moves towards* MARYLIN.

You keep your nose clean, and you can stay. If you can't, you can be off in two hours in a Navy helicopter. And you won't ever get an exit visa again.

Marylin You're bluffing. You're a third-grade flatfoot, stumbling round Paranoia Hall with your fly open.

Clements Lady, I was in Moscow when the Russians bombarded the embassy with radio waves. We all got sick. I go on vacation with the guy who designed plastic shrapnel, so it wouldn't show up in X-rays of wounded in North Vietnam. I don't care if you were voted the most popular girl in your grade, you're going to lie low until we have some positive feedback. And if I can't use the helicopter – (*Shows her his shoulder-holstered modern automatic.*) – I'll use this. (*Breaks from her to left centre.*)

Marylin (*pause, turns on* SYLVIA) Sylvia? What do you think you were doing in the shower?

RITSAAT *enters down the steps.* CLEMENTS *leaves slowly.*

Sylvia For Christ's sake, he was only helping me on with my corset.

Ritsaat What's been happening?

Marylin We've been trying to decide who gets the shiksa.

Carson What was the noise?

Ritsaat Nothing . . . Big portrait fell down in my study. Can we get on? (*Resumes his seat down right.*)

MARKS, WISHBONE *and* LAZARUS *exit upstage.*

Sylvia They made a pile of bodies in the snow. And then the child climbed out of it, covered in blood and doings. So I walked south-west for a thousand miles, with the child sometimes on my back and got to the great plains. There is nothing to see on the great plains, and many people went completely mad. I set up in a turf hut, with a cowboy working casual for McCoys. Later, work became scarce and times grew hard. So I went on the game, and had a little luck with two Englishmen down the road, who gave me some beans. (*Begins washing beans in pan.*)

> BILL *enters from up left.*

Bill Where's the child?
Sylvia I don't know.
Bill What's for supper?
Sylvia Beans.
Bill Is that all, for a man on strike?
Sylvia Yes.

> WILLYA *enters from up left.*

Bill Did you soak 'em? You never soak 'em properly. (*Pause,* BILL *and* WILLYA *see hoof.*) What's that?
Sylvia It's a bit of hoof. I found it in the road.
Bill At least it'll gum the insides together.

> WILLYA *steals the hoof.*

Sylvia Willya! Give it back! (*Takes it from her.*) Where've you been?
Bill The depot. Where did the beans come from?
Sylvia Two Englishmen up the road.
Bill Money?
Sylvia Beans.
Bill Jesus! I could've got fucked for more'n a pan of beans. You say something?
Sylvia Nothing.
Bill Give us a kiss. (*Reaches over.*)

> CLEMENTS *and* CARSON *enter from up right, masked.* SYLVIA *and* WILLYA *break to right.* CARSON *seizes* BILL, *holds gun under his chin.*

Clements Don't move, or he'll repaint your roof. That's the boy who's been leading the strike. We just dropped in to give you a wrist slap. Shoot him in the knees, for now.

> CARSON *aims his gun at* BILL's *knees, and* LAZARUS *in the up right corner, provides the two shots from his starting pistol. The* COWBOYS *leave abruptly.* BILL, SYLVIA *and* WILLYA *exit with the chair, table and props.* MARKS *and* WISHBONE *enter from up left with a camp stool, bed-roll, fire and cooking-pot, knife, Martini, rifle, blankets and a Gladstone bag. They are dressed like a decayed Victorian gentlemen, full camp aroma, all a bit shoddy. They set their props, and* WISHBONE *sits left centre on the stool.* MARKS *stands above the fire and sings 'Early one Morning'. He reaches the end, makes up a bed at left, using two blankets, one rolled as a pillow, the other folded in half.*

Wishbone Well?
Marks Yes, sir?
Wishbone Are you avoiding me?

Marks No, sir.

Wishbone Do I smell?

Marks Yes, sir.

Wishbone What is left in the library?

Marks (*sits left of fire*) One American book, sir. *Moby Dick*. A book about the whaling industry.

Wishbone (*rises*) Never mind that. What are all these bones here?

Marks Buffalo, sir, before the railway. They only shot them for the pelts. (*Cuts up a carrot into cooking-pot.*)

Wishbone I might have known it. I came here to farm sheep. The great plains are ideal for sheep farming. (*Looks at* MARKS.) But no American will farm them, they're afraid of being thought 'yellow'. I'm glad to go back.

MARKS *looks at him, then away.* WISHBONE *looks front.*

I've really had enough. The sky isn't right, for a start. The sun's taking far too long to go down. And you walk and walk and all the time we've been walking back, there's been these streams of grubby people in the other direction, trying to get to San Francisco. So determined. So ugly. And that woman we entertained. What did you give her?

Marks A pound and a half of navy beans, sir.

Wishbone (*above* MARKS *to right*) I'm feeling devilish itchy. D'you think I caught crabs off her?

Marks No, sir. Sir, you had them already, before you met the woman.

Wishbone You had her, too! Why haven't you got them?

Marks Sir, while on vacation, I take the precaution of shaving off all bodily hair.

Wishbone Hardly seems worth it, if a chap's got to lather his bum every morning. I'd just as soon scratch . . . (*Looks front.*) What are those lights in the sky? (*Points*).

MARKS *looks front.*

Are they proof of the existence of God?

Marks As a Darwinian, sir, I'd have to say no, in a roundabout sort of way.

Wishbone Quite: who'd want to hold a conversation with a triangular light? (*Pause.*) I can't talk to Him in front of you. I assume it's me He's interested in. (*Pause.*) That will be all, Marks.

Marks Yes, sir. (*Breaks to up left, behind curtain.*)

WISHBONE *watches him go, looks front. Becomes afraid of the light. Pause. Looks back.*

Wishbone No, don't leave me.

MARKS *returns to centre.*

I'm not going to look till the sky is right. (WISHBONE *looks away to off right.*) Is that a camel?

Marks No, sir, two humps. Dromedary.

Wishbone Give me the Martini.

MARKS *does so, and* WISHBONE *aims.*

I can see the camel, but it's too dark to see the sights.

Marks One moment, sir. (*Lights match by rear sight.*)

Wishbone Hold it. Watch the birdie.

LAZARUS *appears up right, produces a gunshot from his starting pistol. Exits.*

Marks Good shot, sir.

Wishbone Would you take its head off with my razor.

MARKS *collects cut-throat razor from Gladstone bag, dumps knife, exits.*)

Wishbone A camel. I say! In the middle of the great plains! A camel. (*Looks front.*) Thank you God! You're taking your time over the sunset. I'm rather puzzled by there being a camel here. Was it for me? Anyhow, nice to see you. Good night. (*Under blanket.*)

MARKS *re-enters right, replaces the razor in the Gladstone bag, produces a tenon saw.*

That was quick.

Marks I'll need the tenon saw, sir, for the vertebrae.

Wishbone It's a mystery to me. A sign. I mean, am I that important, d'you think?

Marks Well, sir. Nothing like the great plains had ever been seen, so the Army tried bringing in camels to police the area. It was like your sheep, sir. It was treated with such contempt that it just disappeared.

Wishbone We do see things very differently. You see, I know it was meant for me. These buffalo bones were meant for me. Otherwise they would be somewhere else.

Marks Well no, sir. The Indians followed the buffalo. Then came the trader's trace. Then the turnpike. Then the railway. That is why the buffalo bones are near the railway.

Wishbone Good night, Marks.

Marks Good night, sir. (*Replaces saw, sings 'Silent Night' in German.*)

As the song proceeds, WISHBONE *rises, strikes bedding, stool, rifle and Gladstone bag and exits up left.* MARKS *strikes the fire and pot, and exits singing.* MARYLIN *and* SYLVIA *enter from right and left, each with a bentwood chair. They set them at centre, facing each other.* WILLYA *enters down left and sits on the floor.* SYLVIA *sits on left chair.* MARYLIN *between them, facing front.* MARYLIN *in full madame's costume.*

Marylin If this train doesn't move soon, we're going to be burnt to a frazzle. I didn't figure to be caught in the sidings with a lot of roast beef in Ogallalah. This coach is a replica of Queen Victoria's.

Sylvia D'you think we'll get out before the fire comes?

Marylin You picked a good time to leave. The money's not in cowboys any more. How d'you hear of me?

Sylvia I went to the Dewdrop dance-hall on Main Street.

Marylin D'you know where the money is? Minerals. Ogallalah's finished as a railhead town. I'm going to Leadville. The idea of a private coach is to get their first. Offer better entertainment, skim the cream off a boom town, and move on before the regular cathouses set up. (*Pause.*) You have a year or so of bloom. Style is just as important as youth. Just remember you're English – a countess.

Sylvia I couldn't do that.

Marylin The younger sister of Countess Bradshaw, an Honourable in her own right.

Sylvia I don't speak proper.

Marylin What?

Sylvia I don't speak properly.

Marylin Cleft palate?

Sylvia I don't have the right accent.

Marylin Never mind. Just remember you're English. Did you finish with your man?

Sylvia Yes.

Marylin Children?

Sylvia Erm . . . no. (*Pause.*) One. He's looking after her. Normally he works as a cowboy. But he hasn't been able to get work because of the strike. She's just come to say good-bye. (*Kisses* WILLYA *and returns to 'coach'.*)

WILLYA *exits down left.*

Marylin There's a bright side to everything. Sylvia, if you want to make big money – sparkle!

Sylvia Sparkle. . . .

Marylin Yeah – sparkle! I can see you take your colour from your surroundings – so we'll sparkle!

Sylvia Sparkle!

Marylin Sparkle! Chin up. Tell me a joke.

Sylvia (*pause*) There are two boiled eggs in a pan, and one said to the other, 'Bloody hell, it's hot in here.' And the other one said, 'Just you wait till you get outside. They bash your head in.'

Marylin (*pause*) We'll forget that one. And sparkle, Desiree! Rise like a phoenix and . . .

Sounds of a train starting to move.

. . . look! The train's moving! Leadville, here we come! New places! New faces! God loves those who help themselves!

RITSAAT *rises, breaking in once more.*

Ritsaat (*interrupting*) Hold it!

> LAZARUS *enters down right, moves to* RITSAAT, *company wander on.*

Can't you feel it? The tension? The moral vacuum to suck in the Anti-Christ?

> *All look blankly at him.*

He's coming. I want to tell you he's coming – I can feel it in my bones. Some sort of . . . ultra-receptivity. Has anyone noticed anything unusual? Any thick green light anywhere? Anyone's watch going backwards, or stopped?

> *Humouring him, they look.*

Lazarus, can we safely halt here?
Lazarus It's as safe as anywhere else.
Ritsaat Stop it, then, till I come back. (*Exit down right.*)

> MARYLIN *and* SYLVIA *strike their chairs.* WILLYA *enters down left with a bandolier, toy gun and holster.*

Lazarus (*to up right*) OK, Carson, plan 'A' starts. Mrs Hooley, will you keep a lookout?
Mrs Hooley What for?
Lazarus For Ritsaat. Tip us the wink, when you see him.

> CARSON *enters up right, half-carrying* UMBERTO, *who is comatose: a large darkish Spaniard in chef's outfit.* BILL *follows them on.* MRS HOOLEY *moves down right, looks offstage.*

Carson Give me an A! Give me an N! Give me a T! Give me an I! What does it spell? Umberto! (*Dumps him on the floor centre.*)
Brian The gentleman appears to have had a drop taken.
Lazarus Bill, you're the drugs expert. What d'you reckon he's on?
Bill Smells like booze.
Marks Oh, God! I can't work with people who drink.

> BRIAN *and* BILL *put holster on* UMBERTO, *then add the gun.*

Willya (*putting bandolier on* UMBERTO) It's not just drink. We paid him with two bottles of Brian's poteen, but he wanted something else – so Carson gave him pills.
Carson A couple of black bombers. He wanted Willya, but she's not for sale.
Wishbone Clements, you're not going to report this, are you?

> *Pause. All look at* CLEMENTS.

Clements D'you think that's the first time I've seen a stoned gook?
Wishbone Not exactly what I was asking, but I take it you're not. Good. We've got to get him sobered up. Maybe some black coffee. . . .

MARKS *and* WISHBONE *leave to hunt for coffee.*

Mrs Hooley A cup of tea?

WILLYA *exits down left.*

Lazarus Mrs Hooley, just stick to your job, will you?
Marylin At this point, I wash my hands of this. (*Breaks down left.*)

WILLYA *enters down left with sombrero and sandals for* UMBERTO.

Sylvia (*moves to* MARYLIN) Why? We could see if it works.
Willya I think his moustache needs thickening. (*Puts sombrero on him.*)
Brian Did you take *two* bottles of the poteen?
Carson Brian, we've got to drink it some time. You did pinch all our potatoes.
Brian But *two* bottles.

SYLVIA *puts sandals on* UMBERTO.

Carson It was the only way to get him here.
Marks Won't Ritsaat have seen him before?
Carson This lad swore he never came up on deck. And besides, they all look alike, this lot, don't they?
Willya He's the crew's cook.
Wishbone Aren't they going to miss him at tea time?
Marks Are you sure Ritsaat hasn't seen him? You could hardly miss him.
Bill He's not very small, is he? I mean, he doesn't exactly look like one of the little people.
Marylin (*in to them*) You're setting him up to be killed.
Bill I don't think it will work.
Marylin Ritsaat's going to pull a gun on this guy.
Umberto (*rousing*) Companeros . . . que pasa? . . . Companeros?
Marks (*to* CARSON) What's he saying?
Wishbone He's saying he's a member of Cuban Equity.
Carson (*to* MARYLIN) He's got about the same chance as the rest of us of getting out of here alive.
Marylin Not playing the AntiChrist.
Umberto Companeros. . . .
Carson He's from the right part of the world. He's one of Fidel's lads, OK?
Lazarus Enough of this standing around vaporising. Get him into line. I want him to start work right away as one of the cowboys.
Bill He's in no fit state.
Carson I'd wait, if I were you.
Willya Can't I finish making him look good?
Lazarus (*directing them*) We've got to get him in now. He should have been here half an hour ago, instead of getting smashed.
Marks He can't even speak English!

Carson I'll go and get his mate, if you like. Little fat bloke, with a hunchback. He wanted to come, too.

MARKS *and* WISHBONE *pick up* UMBERTO.

Marks What did *he* think he was going to do? Play Richard the Third?
Lazarus Stop talking, you facetious old queens, and get into line.
Marks Talk about the pot calling the kettles black! (*Lets go of his side of* UMBERTO.)

UMBERTO *falls*.

Bill (*points*) Man will never fly.
Mrs Hooley He's coming! He's coming!
Lazarus Make him inconspicuous.
Wishbone How?
Marks There is no way we can do that. Sorry.
Lazarus Put him at the back.
Mrs Hooley He's almost here!

The COWBOYS *are lined up at the back, with* UMBERTO *now supported behind them. Marylin faces them downstage.*

Lazarus Shut up, Kathleen. I'm trying to think!
Mrs Hooley He's here. He is!
Lazarus OK. OK.

RITSAAT *enters down right.*

(*Pause.*) Get out of the way, Marylin. We're going to be using this space.
Ritsaat Something wrong, Marylin?
Lazarus The women aren't in this. This is the *action*.
Ritsaat Cheer up, Marylin. You can't always play Moses.

RITSAAT *sits in his chair down right.* CLEMENTS *rises from bench left, joins line, looks heavily at* MARYLIN *with a gesture towards his shoulder-holster.*

Marylin (*pause*) It is not myself I'm feeling sorry for.

MARYLIN *exits left.* MRS HOOLEY *follows her off.* SYLVIA *and* WILLYA *are up right.*

Ritsaat Women! Right, Lazarus, what have you got for us?
Lazarus Go!

The line surges majestically downstage with a great yell. UMBERTO *falls flat on his face at centre. The* COWBOYS *draw aside to down left. Pause.*

Ritsaat Don't anybody *touch* him!
Carson Cor! Look at that!
Bill I haven't seen him before.

Ritsaat So this is . . . the moment, is it? So this is it. (*Prepares to draw his gun on* UMBERTO.)

UMBERTO *begins to snore.* RITSAAT, *surprised, relaxes his stance.*

Marks Mr Ritsaat, you're not going to attack him, are you? Because if you are. . . .

Ritsaat He's come here to attack *me*! It is written, that the AntiChrist shall have every bone broken in his body. But first, *he's* got to attack *me*.

Wishbone You're not going to provoke him though?

Ritsaat Now, I want you to treat him like a god. Get a chair for him. Put him on it. That's right . . . opposite mine.

A folding chair is fetched, and they prop UMBERTO *up in it at down left.*

Carefully . . . carefully . . . that's it. Treat him with respect. He's tired. He's come a long way. Don't worry about catching his eye . . . you'll probably be no more than shadows to him, in contemporary time . . . the past is always richer than the present life. He'll probably get nasty when he realises he's been tricked into coming here . . . till then, I want you to carry on as if nothing had happened, so he can wake in familiar surroundings. Be his memory. Give him life. (*Resumes his seat.*)

The play resumes.

Bill Cowboys – fellow workers. Do not let this train move. Do not let this cattle train leave the depot. This train was loaded by blacklegs.

SYLVIA *and* WILLYA *pull back the curtains masking the train, strike the props from the front of it, then exit up left.*

(*Breaks from group to centre.*) The official packers and dressers union in Chicago has come out in sympathy with our demands!

Joyful reaction from the crowd. CARSON *collects a crate from under the bench left, sets it centre for* BILL. BILL *stands on it.*

Do not let this train move! Stand firm! The driver will not shed a fellow American's blood needlessly! During this last year the price of cattle has dropped at the railheads from forty-nine dollars in eighteen eighty-five to nine dollars this year. The employers and owners of the railroads and stockyards are making a killing from this meat, which is exported all over the world – on a railway system that Americans built, and is grinding them into the ground. We have had no money from our employers, and even *owe* our employers money, because we have to pay them fifteen dollars a month to hire our boots and hats.

Pause.

You've been told by your employers not to read newspapers, in case you see how wide the disaffection is. And it is wide. It stretches right the way down the Goodnight-Loving trail. It stretches deep into the heart of Texas. There are twenty thousand of us who serve. On the Chisholm trail, the Sedalia trail, the Western trail. You won't read this in a newspaper. If they let you read the newspapers, it's because they own them – and if you can afford one, you won't find a single story about what is really happening here. Equality was conceived in America, but does not yet extend to Negroes, immigrants or cowboys! We are being robbed of an inheritance of wealth, by men who as soon as they have it safely in their grasp are all staunch upholders of the laws of property!

Clements (*interrupting him*) Boys, I hope you realise you're breakin' the law. Much as it grieves me to tell you, this here's Company land. I want you to let this here train leave the depot, and get to Chicago. You've been told that you can't get your share of the pickings here. Well, it just ain't true. You all have the right to seize and call your own any unbranded cattle, and you are allowed to reprieve them under the Maverick Law, which was granted to the Association of Ranchers, to whom all your employers belong –

Bill Yes – and the Associations will do their best to see that we never see unbranded cattle again! The essence of a socialist society is in the fact that the great working mass – that's us – ceases to be a ruled mass, and that it lives and directs the economic and political life in free and conscious self-determination. Do not break the picket line! Do not let the train break strike! I am a patriot. I am not Irish, I am an American. America can set an example to the world. We say that all men are created equal, and yet we deny it every other second of the day. Why is it that the actual producers of wealth get least of it?

BILL *steps down from his crate and throws it under the bench right, as* CLEMENTS *stands on the crate at left centre.*

WISHBONE *and* LAZARUS *join the picket line, leaving* MARKS, BRIAN *and* CARSON *at down left to listen to* CLEMENTS.

Clements Boys, I just can't get used to raising rabble in the style of your man here. Course, he's had some practice. Freedom is an American notion, conceived in the backwoods and frontiers, and celebrating man's status. It is not affected by the lies and theories coming in on every tide like cholera from the ghettoes and hunger-torn areas of Europe. You've been told that America is waiting to hear what Socialism is. You've been told to act in your capacity as proletariat. Proletariat! Now I may be a shoe-shine boy, I may be a horse-shit shoveller. I may be bear-clawed, bear-chawed and bare-assed. I may be low down and sicker'n a fukken dawg, but – 'scuse my French – I ain't no proletariat! That cowboys – that ancient, noble breed of men – can stoop to *union* talk – Cowboys don't belong in *unions*! We all know where cowboys belong! Cowboys belong in *bars*! Saloon's open, boys, and the drinks're on me!

BRIAN *joins the line.*

Bill You've all seen the railheads pushing down to Abilene. It's not an eight-hour job, it's a twenty-four hour job. Unless we stick together out here, we're doomed. We're not shoemakers or lathe operators. (MARKS *and* CARSON *join the pickets.*) But we do want a union, so our members don't get *blackballed.*

Clements (*off crate to down left*) Free liquor, boys. (*Pause.*) And if you walk into the bar with me now, I give my solemn word you don't ever get blackballed. (*Pause to down right.*) We'll just pretend it never happened. (*Pause.*) Carson – are you hungry?

Carson (*unsure*) No.

Clements Pity. I could a sworn I smelt a fry-up, coming out that there bar. (*Sniffs.*)

Carson (*pause: he steps forward*) All right, then – (*Looks at* CLEMENTS.) – how about something to eat?

Clements Sure. I'm grubstakin'.

CARSON *exits down left.* BILL *looks after him.*

Solid American food, not fancy ghetto cooking. Corn on the cob. Pancakes with maple syrup. Hash browns. Steak. 'Course I know all you socialists are vegetarians. . . .

LAZARUS *breaks from the line, exits down left.*

After a hard day on the range, what does the cowboy, that romantic figure, require? *We* got the whisky, *we* got the vittels, and if he's handsome *he* gets the women. Romance!

Bill It's only romantic in so far as we're on the way to getting wiped out, like the Indians. They'll put cowboys in reservations, and then we'll see what happened to your proud independence.

MARKS *and* WISHBONE *exit down left.*

Don't desert me! Don't leave me! (*Looks at* BRIAN.) Two's enough to hold a bridge.

Brian (*pause: begins to waver and drift*) Grieves my heart to abandon a glorious enterprise for bad food and worse whisky – but I ain't ate meat for a month. (*Exits down left.*)

Clements (*moves to left, speaks offstage*) Now you're being sensible, boys. I'll see y'all in there.

BILL *sits on the tracks at down centre, his legs out in front of him.*

I just got to have a word with the driver. (*To up centre.*) Driver! Driver! Tell the driver the line's clear, and move that train.

Bill *I'm* here!

Clements Never mind. Tell the driver the line's clear, move that train! C'mon, train!

CLEMENTS *waves the train on. Lights darken to full ochre. Gouts of steam and smoke. Terrific noises. The train moves forward as the lights dim to blackout. The sound of the train diminishes, and fades into the distance. Lights restore.* BILL *remains seated, with severed legs lying neatly in front of him.* CLEMENTS *facing the audience, his back in shadow.*

Clements You . . . outdoor boy, you . . . glad hand. Well, now – (*Kicks legs aside.*) – that's the way of your standing in the way of progress. If you'll forgive the homely pun.

Bill I shall need a doctor.

Clements What for? For a communist arsonist?

Bill Get me a fukken doctor!

Clements Why don't you run along and get him yourself? You don't get a vet for a dog with rabies. Get that Pope of yours jumping up and down. You're going to need him.

Bill What's the Pope to you or me? Sod the Pope.

Clements With his dying breath he repudiated Catholicism.

CLEMENTS *is struck in the upper back with an arrow. He starts to totter and falls.* WILLYA *appears out of the shadows up right with her bow and a handcart.*

Bill Quick! Get me downtown! I need a doctor. (*Picks up legs.*)

She helps him on to the cart.

Bloody great train ran over me. What's happened to the Sheriff?

Willya I killed him. (*Starts to push him towards up right.*) There's no-one in Ogallalah – it's on fire.

Bill No, not that way. That's to the plains. The other door.

WILLYA *is still pushing.*

Willya Ogallalah is *burning.*

Bill (*resigned*) Oh. All right?

WILLYA *and* BILL *exit up right.* CARSON *enters up left with* BRIAN *and* MRS HOOLEY *on the end of a rope.* CLEMENTS *gets up slowly, shaking himself.*

Clements What the hell are you doing, Carson? Oh, yes, we was hanging the Irish. Plumb forgot about it.

Carson Boss, are you all right?

Clements (*shows him the arrow*) See that? I'm going to find out who's responsible for this.

They all start to trudge off down right, with CLEMENTS *leading.*

Does that look like a Sioux?

Carson No.

Clements Cree?

Carson No.

Clements Arrapaho?
Carson No.
Clements Blackfoot.
Carson No.
Clements Cheyenne?
Carson No.
Clements Well, what *does* it look like? (*Exits.*)
Carson Looks like an arrow to me. (CARSON *exits and* HOOLEYS.)

> RITSAAT *and* UMBERTO *are left alone on stage, on their chairs.* UMBERTO *asleep.*

Ritsaat I'd just like to say . . . about the duel . . . not personal, the emnity . . . (*Rises towards* UMBERTO.) I expect you know all about me. I draw at about point-thirty-five. I expect you're pretty fast, in this incarnation. Welcome aboard. It was you, wasn't it, who put poison in the Führer's begel, to warn him against Zionist bakers? Just checking. Must have been while he was living in the Fögelstrasse.

> MARKS *and* WISHBONE *enter up left and begin to set their props.*

Anything I can get you?

> UMBERTO *wakes and looks up. In a flash,* RITSAAT *draws.* UMBERTO *stands and looks about him in amazement.* RITSAAT *relaxes a little and holsters his gun.* UMBERTO *yawns and stretches.*

Feel free to go wherever you want. No-one will refuse you anything. I'll be around. Come back to the action when you feel the time is right.

> UMBERTO *turns, exits down left.* RITSAAT *follows to down left, practises his draw once or twice.* LAZARUS *enters up left.*

Marks I say, Ritsaat. There's no point in carrying on if Anti-er-Christ isn't here, is there?
Wishbone It's a bit like a Royal Command Performance without the Queen.
Ritsaat No, no – you must continue. Don't you see, the play is breathing life into him. Energy. Soon he must return, and I will be ready for him. Lazarus, what happens next?
Lazarus Marylin and Sylvia arrive on the train.
Ritsaat Good, good. That should stimulate him.

> LAZARUS *exits down left.*

Marks (*still nervous from* RITSAAT's *brush with* UMBERTO) I don't know if I've got stage fright, or not –
Wishbone Probably just ordinary terror.
Ritsaat Come on, chaps – we must get on.

> RITSAAT *resumes his seat down right.* MARKS *and* WISHBONE *resume their characters.* WISHBONE *gets into 'bed', and* MARKS *produces an elegant*

teacup and saucer from the Gladstone bag, shaking with fright until into character.

Marks Good morning, sir.

Wishbone Was there no trains during the night?

Marks No sir. Industrial action at the railhead disrupted normal service.

> WISHBONE *rises, and accepts the cup of tea from* MARKS, *sipping it as he speaks.*

Wishbone Well that's what happens, isn't it, as soon as you give people – (*Wanders down left with his tea.*) – their freedom. That's the trouble with America. The country is enslaved by one idea. Freedom.

> WILLYA *and* BILL *appear up right, moving to down right.* BILL *still in the cart.*

Willya Mister. Quick. Medicine.

Wishbone (*oblivious*) And complete freedom means freedom also from taste. From civilisation. In fact – anarchy.

Marks (*making a hasty examination*) I must sew those veins up immediately. (*Collects Gladstone bag, brings it downstage to them.*)

Wishbone (WISHBONE *sees* BILL) Who is he?

Marks I don't know, sir.

Bill Will the patient live?

Marks He came out of the plains with the child. (*Opens bag, produces a needle and cotton.*) I'll round the end off, and tuck a flap of skin over the stump.

Bill I've got a couple of buttons missing, as well.

> MARKS *produces a flask of whisky from the bag, hands it to* BILL, *who accepts it gratefully.*

Marks This may hurt.

Bill Ta. I don't mind pain. I can't just stand the threat of it. (*Drinks.*)

Marks It's all in the mind.

Bill Thank you.

> MARKS *begins sewing his left leg.*

(*Pause: drink.*) Tell me: you're an educated man. What are those lights in the sky? Always seeing them, when I'm on the trail at night – settling on hillsides, coming – whoosh! – out of quiet lakes. What do they mean? Lights. More and more lights.

Marks (*finishes sewing the right leg*) Poor fellow. I think this is the end for him.

Willya Put legs . . . back on.

Marks No, it's hopeless. The femurs are crushed.

Willya (*trying to push them on*) Legs . . . back on.

Wishbone Does the child believe in miracles? She keeps pushing his legs on again.

Willya Not a miracle. Seen it done. At a medicine show!

Marks I can't do it. I can't make him whole again.

Wishbone Are you Indian?

Willya Half.

Wishbone Why aren't you on your reservation? The Indian Nations. . . .

The sound of a train approaching. MARKS *listens.*

Marks Sir, I think I hear a train coming.

Wishbone I say! Pack up, quick.

MARKS *begins moving their gear to the down right corner.*

I don't mean any disrespect for your dead father, but I've just got to get out of here, and have a bath and some decent conversation.

Marks (*at down right with the first load*) I'm sorry. There's nothing more I can do. I'm afraid your father is as good as dead. (*Collects the fire and cooking pot, moves them down right.*)

CLEMENTS *enters up left still with arrow with* CARSON *trailing* BRIAN *and* MRS HOOLEY. WILLYA *hides with* BILL *under a blanket.* CLEMENTS *moves to centre.*

Clements Are you Communists? Are you anything to do with the cowboy strike. Did you set fire to Ogallalah?

Marks No.

Clements You're not Communist saboteurs?

Wishbone Do we look like freethinkers or Communists? We pay for everything we take. My name is Sir Charles Wishbone – at your service. (*Sips his tea.*)

Clements Well, I'll be a suck-egg mule! Name's Clements. I'm Sheriff round here. There's been a cowboys' strike, and we've finally got to the bottom of it. It's them Irish Communists been fermenting trouble all along.

Wishbone I see.

BRIAN *and* MRS HOOLEY *move slightly downstage.*

Clements Have these people stolen anything from you, your Dukeship?

Wishbone I don't think so.

Clements Their son was the man leading the strike. But he got his legs cut off by a train, and he's run off. You haven't seen a legless man around here anywhere, have you?

Wishbone (*about to say 'yes'*) Er . . .

Marks No.

Clements Well, that's it, your Dukedom. Sorry to disturb you at this time of the morning. Thought you was vagrants. (*Moves down left.*)

Mrs Hooley (*stopping their procession*) Wait! There was a Charles Wishbone owned Hooley Island.

Brian It's the same man, but he's promoted himself. You fukken bastard. (*Tries to get to* WISHBONE.)

Wishbone What?

Brian You're no more a Lord than my arsehole is. You sold Hooley Island to the military. English! Traitor!

Mrs Hooley You shelled us out of house and home! You Peelite! Our son will avenge us on you! Wherever he is!

BILL *pushes back the blanket.*

Mrs Hooley Bill! My son!

Bill (*flat*) Mother? I could have done without this.

Mrs Hooley You're a hard man to please, Bill. (*Embraces him.*)

Clements (*drawing his revolver, pushes* MRS HOOLEY *off* BILL) Now quiet, all of you. This is the most wanted man in the whole territory, and he just happened to be under this wrap. How in hell did you get here?

Bill Wheelbarrow.

Wishbone This body is nothing to do with me.

Clements That may very well be, but I'm going to take you all in till I find out what's happened. We'll all get on this here train – (*Points front.*) – and go back to Ogallalah, so you all put your hands in the air and surrender your weapons.

They raise their hands, WISHBONE *still holding his teacup.* LAZARUS *enters from upstage in full bordello drag outfit, with wig, and carrying a rifle.*

Lazarus Hands up yourself, Sheriff! *I've* got the drop on *you*, this time.

All valiantly remain in character. CLEMENTS *drops his gun, and* WILLYA *pops up from behind the cart.*

Willya Mummy! (*Moves towards* LAZARUS.)

Lazarus Willya! (*Meets her at centre.*)

WILLYA *and* LAZARUS *are about to embrace.*

Clements Just a minute. The kid with the bow and arrow was. . . .

RITSAAT *jumps up and moves to centre, interrupting once more. The company relaxes.*

Ritsaat What's going on? Lazarus, what are you doing dressed up like a dog's dinner? Where are Marylin and Sylvia? This is disgusting.

Lazarus Well, Rits. . . . Marylin refused to take any further part on dialectic grounds, and Sylvia is trying to find her, so I thought I should step into the breach. The show must go on.

Ritsaat This is very dangerous. Don't you realise what you're *doing*? God knows what will happen now. I should never have let him out of my sight. I must follow him and knock him off, before anything else happens. The Stock Exchange will be going wild! You lot stay here. I've got to get him before we get holed by a Russian submarine. Nobody's to leave. It could be very dangerous. (*Exits down left with automatic drawn.*)

Lazarus Really, this is impossible! I've put a lot of effort into this.

Marks I must say, Lazarus, if the others were off I thought it very professional of you to step in.

Carson Somebody had better find Umberto, before Ritsaat does something nasty to him.

Willya Where's mummy gone?

Bill Don't you worry. She'll survive.

Mrs Hooley I don't like to think of them out there, with that big fellow stalking about.

Lazarus Don't worry – I'll find them. I've got Umberto's speech for him, too. *If* he can sober up. (*Exits up right.*)

Carson Yeah, and if you can teach him English.

Wishbone I'm not going on with him if he's drunk, and that's final.

Willya Ssh. Quiet, everybody. Listen.

They all listen. Silence.

Brian (*pause*) What is it?

Willya Nothing.

Bill (*pause*) She's right. There's no noise. The engine's stopped.

Pause. They all look at each other. Pause. Blackout.

In the blackout, the shower unit and backing are flown in, and the benches, rostrum and steam vent are set as before.

SCENE 2

The shower-room.

Steam, as before. In the set, SYLVIA *entering pushed by* UMBERTO.

Sylvia No, Umberto, I don't think. . . . It's the wrong time of the month.

Umberto Take your clothes off.

Sylvia I can't love. I've got another scene in a minute.

UMBERTO *hits her. She begins to undress.* LAZARUS *enters centre, from right.* SYLVIA *looks up at him.*

Sylvia Can you help me? Please!

Lazarus (*ploughing into* UMBERTO) See here, fella, you can take fun and games too far. You may think you're the cat's pyjamas in that outfit, but we put you in it. Inside that greasy skin of yours, all there is, is a whole lot of liquor and a Hispanic cook. (*Pushes him down to bench right.*) You don't fool me, sailor. We made you. (UMBERTO *draws a revolver, points it at* LAZARUS.) That's just a toy gun. We give you the sign to move, so sit down and learn that speech. (*Thrusts a speech into* UMBERTO's *hand.*) I put the words into your mouth –

Instantly, UMBERTO *fires and blows* LAZARUS's *brains out, Blood and brains splatter over the shower curtain.* LAZARUS's *body falls into shower.* CLEMENTS, *catatonic once more, enters centre from right, sits on the steam vent.* UMBERTO *returns his attentions to* SYLVIA.

Umberto We go to a bunk. It's too crowded in here.

UMBERTO *exits centre with* SYLVIA, *to right.* CLEMENTS's *blanket caked with snow.*

Clements So . . . cold. Snow's coming . . . just like it was when . . . hey . . . (*Turns to* LAZARUS.) I know you, boy. I know you. Don't I?

Blackout. Shower unit and backing fly out, and furniture is struck.

SCENE 3

The hold once more.

Lights up. The stage and company as they were, plus MARYLIN *at the top of the steps.*

Marylin OK you pack of assholes. We've run out of oil, and the crew have abandoned ship. They got in a panic, and the final straw came when Umberto disappeared. So here's our chance, if we can get ourselves together before Ritsaat steps in. Willya: go and find your mother.

WILLYA *exits up right.*

And Carson, see if you can get Lazarus.

CARSON *exits down left.*

And you'd better find that CIA creep, as well. Everyone else, get your things as quick as you can.

Marks I know it's going to sound stupid, but did we ever unpack the galoshes?
Wishbone I don't know.

MARKS *and* WISHBONE *exit up right.*

Mrs Hooley Brian. Come on. We'd better be quick, now.
Brian Yes, I suppose so. It always ends like this, doesn't it?
Mrs Hooley What do you mean?
Brian Butlins or Switzerland, as soon as you've got a nice store built up, you have to leave.
Mrs Hooley Never mind. Come on, now.

BRIAN *and* MRS HOOLEY *exit down left.* BILL *is by the bench right, massaging his legs.*

Bill What a bloody mess, eh? Me legs have gone to sleep in that last frigging scene – it's agony.

MARYLIN *down steps to left centre.*

Look, if we're going to have to spend six months in a lifeboat together, don't you think we could start off by being civil?

Marylin I can't be civil to you.

Bill She'd never have survived without me.

Marylin You sent her out to whore for you.

Bill We got good money for it. You see, I love her for herself. She doesn't need your 'education' for me to love her. It doesn't make any difference in the end.

Marylin Doesn't it?

Bill It's feelings which count. (SYLVIA *enters right, supported by* WILLYA.) You'll see. In the end, she'll come back to me. (*To centre.*) So who's it to be, Sylvia? That woman or me? I've got the kid – you know that.

When the cast re-enter, they wear a strange combination of their own clothes and the costumes from the Cowboy Play.

Willya Mummy's been raped.

Marylin (*crossing to them*) Who by?

Sylvia (*sits down right*) Umberto. Didn't you hear me screaming? And he's killed Lazarus.

Willya It's awful.

Marylin Whose fucking idea was it to give him two bottles of whisky? Because it's their responsibility.

Sylvia Where were you? Didn't you hear me screaming?

Willya It's awful. There's blood all over the place.

RITSAAT *enters from up right, to down right via up left centre.* BILL *moves to his left.*

Ritsaat Better get her an abortion quick. She's been impregnated by the AntiChrist. I came on them while they were f. . . . I thought I could shoot him before he finished. I blew half his neck away, but of course that only precipitates emission. Sylvia, I don't want you to under-estimate the importance of getting rid of it. For the future of the world. However strongly you may feel you want another child.

Sylvia It's all right – I'm on the pill.

Marylin What! Even when you were with me?

Sylvia It's just as bloody well isn't it?

Ritsaat I've lost him. I think I killed him all right, but he rolled down the steps and fell into the bilges. It's all filth and crude oil down there. I opened the sea-cocks to try and flush him out, so I'm afraid the boat is filling with water. And I want to tell you, the water in the Bermuda

Triangle has a mind all of its own. I must get back to him. (*Exits up right.*)

Marylin It's no good, is it?

Willya What?

Marylin Keeping your mouth shut against your better judgement.

CARSON *enters left, supporting* CLEMENTS. *Sits him in the chair down left.*

Carson Is it true the boat's sinking?

Marylin Yes – How's Clements?

Carson I think he's sinking, an' all. He must have had a heart attack or something. It's not *my* fault. *I* didn't do anything.

MARYLIN, SYLVIA *and* WILLYA *begin a slow progress towards the steps up centre.*

Sylvia I feel very shaky. Do we have to go in the lifeboat now?

Marylin The boat is sinking. Do you have anything to collect?

Carson (*about to join the exodus*) I was going to leave the speakers, anyway. The old toothbrush was wearing down a bit.

Bill Clements is dead.

Pause. He feels CLEMENTS.

His heart's stopped.

Marylin Try the kiss of life.

Carson Me?

Marylin Yeah.

Carson Why me? Why not you?

Bill You're the doctor round here. Get on with it, Carson.

CARSON *kneels by* CLEMENTS, *blows in his mouth.*

Willya (*pause, he works away*) It may not be the right time to tell you, but Carson and me have got engaged.

Sylvia As long as you're both happy, love.

Carson (*pause: rise*) I think he wants to be gone, now.

A groan from CLEMENTS.

Marylin Hey! No!

Clements (*sepulchral pause*) There is mother under the oleanders . . . there is someone there with her . . . open the windows, it's getting dark . . . (*Dies.*)

Carson (*investigates*) He's dead, *now*. (*Breaks to right centre.*)

Bill Cause of death, Doctor Carson?

Carson I don't know, man – I dunno. Maybe he really is time-travelling. He was always saying they wanted to get rid of him. Well, I think *they* sent him back – but it's a one-way ticket. Yeah, that's it. That's my diagnosis. The CIA killed him. (*Sees* CLEMENTS'S *watch.*) That's a laugh. He's got one of those underwater watches on. Just the job for his next posting.

SYLVIA *and* MARYLIN *move to the base of the steps, as* MARKS *and* WISH-BONE *enter up right carrying smart, matching luggage. They move to up centre.*

Marks Has Clements finally succumbed?
Bill (*nods, points to* CLEMENTS) There's your man. Cause of death unknown.
Wishbone Oh, dear. Does anyone know why the boat is sinking?
Bill Gravity.
Marks I see. Did we get into a very strong field of it?
Bill Just the same as it always it. Pulls you down.

RITSAAT *enters down right, carrying a chain-saw.*

Ritsaat It's all right, everybody. Everything's fine. The water is rising quickly now, so he must float out soon. I brought this chain-saw along, so that when he does I can quickly and easily break every bone in his body.

MRS HOOLEY *and* BRIAN *enter down left with their battered cases.*

Mrs Hooley Ah, Mr Ritsaat. We didn't want to leave without saying good-bye.
Brian Thanks very much for having us along, Mr Ritsaat. It's been a pleasure to serve you.
Ritsaat What?
Sylvia Come on, Willya. I'll buy you a nice ring when we get to Cuba. Marylin – come on!
Ritsaat But nobody is to leave until I've set his spirit free. The AntiChrist still stalks the boat.
Mrs Hooley Now don't be silly, Mr Ritsaat. It'll only end in tears, like it did in Switzerland.

The lights flicker, and some go out.

It's time to leave, now. Our bunks were practically awash.
Brian (*on steps*) Please don't misunderstand her, Mr Ritsaat. We'll look after you yet, if we're in the same lifeboat.
Bill There *is* only one lifeboat.
Brian Come along, Kathleen.

BRIAN *makes his progress up the steps, but his suitcase bursts open, showering dozens of apples down on to the stage.* MRS HOOLEY *rushes to his rescue once more.*

Mrs Hooley Leave them!

She takes the empty case from him, throws it down, and hands him a full one. She follows BRIAN *up the steps.*

Go on, Brian! And you, too, Bill – or you'll get your feet wet.

Ritsaat You can't leave now – I absolutely forbid it! It would be highly irre-
sponsible.

Marylin For Christ's sake, Ritsaat – the boat is sinking!

Ritsaat That's just another pathetic excuse for your behaviour, isn't it? All
of you . . . (*With a maniacal sweeping gesture of the chain-saw blade
around the room.*) . . . shiftless drifters, the sweepings of the streets. Ach!
What do you care if the world goes up in flames?

Marylin For fuck sake – there *is* no AntiChrist!

Ritsaat Don't be ridiculous!

Marylin A man was bribed with drink! It was the ship's cook we set on you!

Pause. The cat is out of the bag.

Marks (*pause*) We didn't want to fall short of your expectations.

Wishbone It was just a play, wasn't it?

Marylin I should never have got involved.

Ritsaat I didn't expect you to understand.

Marylin Fucking male fantasies!

MARYLIN *leaves up the steps.*

Ritsaat If we want to know the truth about the past, we've got to go back
there, in 3-D, to the roots of the problem. To smell the slaveships three
tides out in the Bristol Channel; to watch Hitler's peculiar brilliance at
entertaining small children – everywhere where evil resides. There is so
much ground to cover.

RITSAAT *turns to* CARSON, *at right.*

What is happening? Carson, you understand these things. I once heard
of a bloke who slowed a tape recorder down a couple of hundred times,
after he left it in an empty room. And when he did, he heard the millions
of broken phrases in every language and voice – the polyglot babble of
the perpetual underworld. I wanted to invent something better: a
necroscope. A telescope for spying on the dead. So you wouldn't have to
trust to words: you could see for yourself if he was there. Get him in the
sights and – bang! – no words. . . .

CARSON, *having edged round upstage of* RITSAAT, *makes his escape.*
RITSAAT *turns to* BILL *for support.*

Don't trust words. They get up and walk away from you. All axioms are
maxims, but not all maxims are axioms. A Maxim is also the name for a
water-cooled machine-gun, used for polishing off the Indians, whose
own maxim it was that the land belonged to the great Father, stretched
for ever, and could be given to no-one. The Maxim, firing at a bullet a
second . . . (*Demonstrating with the chainsaw.*) . . . pom! pom! pom! –
disproved these narrow assumptions about infinity, space and time –
these three *maxims.*

The lights flicker again, and more go out. Shouts of 'Bill!' are heard from above from the HOOLEYS.

I think I'm losing control. (*Dumps chainsaw at right.*) Well – aren't you going to respond to the popular appeal?

Bill (*by* CLEMENTS'*s body*) I'm taking his Rolex Oyster. Fat chance we have of being paid for this. (*Removes his watch and pockets it.*)

Ritsaat Don't they realise what they've missed? If you look at the world through the eyes of children, anything is possible – even the Man in the moon. Children see things right, because they keep what they want to see alive by the strength of their belief. (*Shouts of 'Bill!' above. Then a hollow crash as a hatch shuts. Lights even darker.*)

BILL *moves towards the steps, so* RITSAAT *addresses the inert body of* CLEMENTS. BILL, *unseen, draws a 'real' gun from a shoulder-holster.*

The world exists as it does because people believe it to be so. Theories of matter last, on average, ten years. I'm not fooled. (*Turns front.*) Between you and your perceptions is the mirror which you think reflects reality.

We see a huge black glistening figure atop the steps. Magnificent. Operatic. BILL *sees him, but* RITSAAT *does not.*

But you can reach out and point it in any direction you like. The world is convertible. By *belief.*

Umberto (*top of steps*) Hey, Mister. . . .

RITSAAT *freezes, unable to turn.*

Stranger . . . ain't I seen your face before? Ain't you a troublemaker? Disruptin' property? Molestin' women? Draw. I shall count to three. (*Draws gun, aims at* RITSAAT.) One . . .

RITSAAT *turns, drawing. Both* UMBERTO *and* BILL *empty their guns into* RITSAAT, *who falls dead.* UMBERTO *descends two steps,* BILL *ascends two. Their arms reach out and their fingers touch. Blackout. A blinding flash. Pause. Flutter of wings, loud. Lights to half, growing to full.* BILL *and* UMBERTO *break tableau and come down the steps as the rest of the cast come on to take their bow. Music, 'Yellow Brick Road'.*

END OF PLAY

AFTERWORD

I have lived with the Hooley family in this play for a number of years since its inception, or their arrival, and I really am very pleased to see them go, as it were, with their cruelty, their clannish ignorance, and their son Bill who changed his name, but was recognisably very much of them, with a cold, plebian exploitation of everyone, particularly the women, within his reach. I kept on the Hooleys not because I thought that the world had a shortage of Irish jokes but because I couldn't get rid of them. In the play there is a sour combat between the failures of democracy and the lunacies of fascism, and *pace* the Hooleys. It is therefore meant to be if not a history, then at least a mirror of the world. In which of course, the Hooleys are central.

I wish I could have had five pounds for every time a lazy critic called a play of mine 'zany' because despite the word's respectable pedigree as a Venetian corruption of *Giovanni*, the servant in *commedia dell'arte*, it suggests, in the mouths of English critics, a condescending nod towards amusements which do not engage the heart and mind, that are, somehow, not to do with them. I would almost rather have the back-handed compliment paid by one of the papers whose correspondent abandoned any attempt to follow the play, to publicise his failure to make an anagram out of my name. I should not want to prevent even this tortuous means of keeping myself in the public eye: there is, however, a need for proper dramatic criticism which is a few cuts above jack-in-a-box facetiousness.

I *am* serious about my work because it tries to describe the world as complex, different and awesome, but also as the same world which prosaic people, or some critics and all Hooleys drag their mind-and-environment-forged manacles around in. Blake formed the idea of mind-forged manacles (before the 'environment' became an acceptable concept) and his pet hate was 'Single vision and Newton's sleep'. The ocean of Truth beside which Newton claimed to have found merely a pebble, has now shifted and expanded and taken back the pebble. But although we cannot accept any more the nineteenth-century fictions about matter, we continue to abide by them, as if the alternative is dreadful to contemplate. Perhaps it is, but if we do not shrink from a world permanently on the brink of nuclear war because of an alleged incompatability between two 'systems' of materialism, and we do not mind the idea of destroying the planet in order to save it, then the *lacuna* in materialism which I have included in this work of the imagination should not cause much difficulty in apprehension.

It would suggest that the audience is an onlooker into the affairs of a group of people all of whom have their own ideas of how the world works and how they fit into it. But the idea is not for the author simply to describe how people are trapped in or transcend their destinies or sensibilities, but to try and make a world as much like the 'real' one as possible. I *don't* mean naturalism by this, but more a sense of the way people's own apprehensions of themselves and the world are both plastic. What I mean is that the play is full of the kind of acts and coincidences which used to be thought of as conveniences of the artistic imagination, but which can, of course, happen in what I must call 'real' life, in spite of the dangers of being misunderstood.

I would like to thank all the actors at the Royal Shakespeare Company who took part in the original workshop, of whom Manning Redwood remained to take his place in the Royal Court production, to play the part of Clements. Appropriately enough for the production, Manning discovered the historical existence of a sheriff in Wyoming in 1886 (which was what he played) called Manning Clements. The cast of the Royal Court production were excellent and the director Max Stafford-Clark wonderfully exact and sedulous when I had lost my way in a wilderness of drafts.

Snoo Wilson